Cinco de Mayo
The Fighting Women of Mexico

Michael Black

ZAMIZ PRESS

Categories: FICTION > WESTERN
FICTION > WAR & MILITARY

Special discounts are available on quantity purchases by corporations, associations and others. For details, contact the author.

DO YOU HAVE A MESSAGE TO SHARE WITH THE WORLD?
ARE YOU INTERESTED IN HAVING YOUR BOOK PUBLISHED?
VISIT ZAMIZ PRESS PUBLISHING AT ZAMIZPRESS.COM.

Cinco de Mayo: The Fighting Women of Mexico — 1st Edition
ISBN: 978-1-949813-10-4
ISBN: 978-1-949813-11-1

Contents

Chapter 1 1

Chapter 2 9

Chapter 3 15

Chapter 4: New Home, August 28, 1859 21

Chapter 5: Pica Diablo 25

Chapter 6: Friends and Enemies 31

Chapter 7: An Army of Peasants 37

Chapter 8: Gun Powder, Chili Powder,
Blood and Lead 39

Chapter 9: The Cannons Roar 43

Chapter 10: Brothers and Sisters of Arms 47

Chapter 11: The Surrender 51

Chapter 12: Mercy and Quarter 59

Chapter 13: Jean Pierre and Juanita 63

Chapter 14: The Prison 67

Chapter 15: Rabble Robbers 71

Chapter 16: Lupe Returns to Caldera 75

Chapter 17: Oso Negro 79

Chapter 18: The Proposal 87

Chapter 19: Children of the Witch 91

Chapter 20: Rancho Martinez de Caldera............. 99

Chapter 21: Paris, France..................................... 103

Chapter 22: Welcome Home................................ 109

Chapter 23: The Guests....................................... 115

Chapter 24: The Big News................................... 121

Chapter 25: No Good Can Come of This............. 125

Chapter 26: The New Discovery.......................... 129

Chapter 27: The Final Chapter............................ 133

About the Author 139

More by Michael Black 141

CHAPTER 1

Vicente Martinez smiled as he passed. He was leading a fifteen-hundred-pound Brahma. The bull's massive muscles undulated, shifting and balancing as it seemed to prance by. She longed for another glimpse of Vicente's eyes, when the bull's hoof landed on her foot. Her scream carried the violence out of her from deep within. She bolted upright in bed. Her sister, asleep under the same covers, was startled awake and joined her screaming.

Erriberto jumped up and flung away the serape that separated his bed from the bed of his daughters.

"What is it?"

"My toe, Papi! My toe!" Lupe cried.

He threw back the cover and found a small orange and yellow scorpion. Grabbing a piece of firewood, he flicked the dangerous creature onto the floor and smashed its head. He lovingly inspected the small round bitemark on his daughter's foot.

"It will be swollen, meja, and will hurt for a few days, then it will go away. You will be well." He touched her cheek with the palm of his calloused hand and patted her sister's silky black hair. "Go back to sleep."

"Go back to your homes," he called to the neighbors who had gathered at his door in response to the screams. "It was only a scorpion in the girl's bed."

Lupe's foot stung from the bite, but she was tired and nuzzled back into her mattress of sweet-smelling grass. Soon she would be dreaming of Vicente again, she hoped.

Her swollen, black and purple foot would not keep her from going out early with her father. Today was an important day for their village. The bull was coming. More important to Lupe, the young, handsome son of the bull master was coming.

A year to the day had passed since the first time the bull had come to Caldera. A tiny pueblo, Caldera consisted of three dozen adobe casitas nested against the base of the Mountains de Sangria del Christo. The name came from the thirsty ravines that carried water of the first spring rain. At that time, they came alive with flowers of vivid red, appearing as if someone had spilled blood on the mountain's summit that ran down toward the village.

Most of Caldera's casitas had only one large room divided with serapes when privacy was desired. Two hundred forty souls made Caldera home. There was a strong, genuine sense of community. Recently, Lupe's father had acquired two cows. It was these two animals who put Caldera on the map.

The bull, coming for the second time, was from the hacienda of Don Escobedo. This Spanish land grant was forty-one thousand acres of timber and rich soil near the city of Queretaro in the state of Guanajuato. They were a three week's caravan north of Mexico City. Most pueblos paid tribute in some form to Don Escobedo. Caldera was too poor and remote. No one went there, until now. Now Caldera had two cows. Only Don Escobedo was entitled to have a bull. His bull alone, could impregnate the cows in the pueblos within his province. Half the calves that resulted became his property.

Lupe recalled every moment from the first time she had seen Vicente. His father had led a massive bull through the pueblo. She remembered the ring through the beast's nose. Then she had seen Vicente as he walked on the opposite side of the slobbering beast. She could see that the boy was keenly aware of each move the bull made. His wore buckskin pants, a printed shirt, leather boots and a felt sombrero de caballero. His colorful bandana hung across his shoulders and onto his back. He contrasted with the near-naked local boys. They wore rough cotton clothes. Their white teeth contrasted their brown faces, shaded by thatched straw hats.

Even at this age, Vicente looked like a man. He had a knife on his belt. A braided lash hung from this wrist, nearly touching the ground. He had glanced her way with a little smile. In the flicker of an eye, she had fallen into the abyss created by the desires felt by a girl who was becoming a woman.

Today the men of Caldera gathered excitedly, waiting at the corral with the cows and the two calves from last year's breeding. Lupe played with a group of children at the mouth of the trail leading to the village. Everyone waited anxiously for the arrival of the bull. It was nearly noon when they heard the rifle-fire that reported the caravan was within earshot. Twenty minutes passed before a cloud of dust was visible on the horizon. Then another thirty minutes ticked by before the cart approached the village. A dozen menacing riders flanked the cart at the head of the herd of steers, collected so far.

Lupe's heart raced, flushed with anticipation.

Would *he* be with them?

As the riders came close enough to examine their faces, her heart sank. Vicente's father rode at the head of the procession, but the face which met her in her dreams, was not among them. Her eyes stung with tears as the cart passed by. Lupe looked down at the dirt to hide her disappointment. The bull was tied to the rear and next to it, on a small black horse, was Vicente. His eyes sparkled and his teeth flashed bright white when he smiled down at her and tipped his hat.

He remembers me.

Once again, the world as Lupe dreamt it, became perfect.

The children followed the dust cloud behind the procession to the corral. The caballeros swung their aching bodies off their horses, stretching their legs and one dropped a branding iron into the fire. The men of Caldera had a fire hot and ready for the procession. The caballeros entered the corral to examine the two calves. They lassoed the baby bull and dragged him into the center.

At fifteen years old, Vincente was nearly six feet tall. He wrestled the rear legs with one arm and front legs with the other. He threw the calf to the ground, on its side. One of the caballeros sat on the calf's head and another sat its body. Vicente's blade glinted in the sunlight as he knelt, and the bull calf became a steer. He placed the testicles in a wooden bowl with a lid. They put the white-hot branding iron to the wound, cauterizing the castration. Then onto the animal's hip, branding it as Don Escobedo's property. As soon as the steer was released, he ran to his mother's side.

Vicente's spurs jangled as he walked to where Lupe stood. "Hola, Lupita."

Her name sounded like a song on his lips.

"Hola, Vicente."

Lupita didn't want to stare, so they watched Senor Martinez lead the bull to one of the cows. The massive bull's front hooves flew up and his hind ones left the ground, kicking pebbles and dirt as he made high leaps, performing the duty he had been brought for.

"Do you ride the bull?" One of the village boys turned to Vincente with wide eyes.

"My father doesn't allow anyone to ride El Saltador, but I ride the other bulls at the rancho," he said, all the while looking at Lupe.

"Your little heifer will be ready to breed next year," Vicente said.

"Si. Then she will be big enough."

"If you get three calves and two are boys and one is a heifer, we will take both the boys. If there are two heifers and one boy, we will only take the boy and leave both heifers."

"What if we get three heifers?" she inquired.

"Then your father will be a very lucky man." He smiled at Lupe. "We will brand one and leave all three here with you."

"I'll pray to the Blessed Virgin that we get at least two girls," Lupe said in a half whisper.

"You are as smart as you are pretty," Vicente replied. As he looked down his tone changed. "What happened to your foot?"

"Un escorpión."

"Oh, Dios mío. Did you kill it?"

"Papa did."

"Good for him. Have the Federales come to your pueblo?"

"No, no one ever comes here. Papa says Caldera is not a stop on the road leading anywhere and Caldera is nowhere to go."

"It's not so bad. Matter of fact, I like it here. You have a good well with sweet water, a little river nearby and a few good trees. The mountains that give shade in the evening.

"Yes, these are true."

"The Federales are enlisting men for the army, men my age. I think I should join but my father says he needs me to help him with the bulls. They can't take anyone from our rancho unless Senor Escobedo, says it's fine. He is very powerful in the government. Did you know that?"

"No. Not until you told me. Now I know," she said and smiled. "Are you coming to the fiesta to bless the cows tonight? Mama and I are cooking. I make the tortillas," she said proudly.

"Can she cook these?" He said, removing the lid and extending the wooden bowl containing the bloody balls of flesh.

"We cook the goat's *huevos*. We can cook these," Lupe said.

"Good, take them. I'll see you tonight. I must go now and help my father." He turned away and then walked purposefully back.

"How old are you?"

"Thirteen, almost fourteen," she replied.

"That's good."

"Why is that good?"

"My father says a man should be at least two years older than his woman."

Lupe's heart swelled until she thought she would burst from joy. She felt as if she had come to realize the reason for her existence. At that moment, she became what she was destined to be, *his woman*.

CHAPTER 2

"Here," Vicente's father tossed a bottle of toilet water. "Put a little of this in your hair. Not too much."

"This might be the most important night of my life," the young man spoke these words in a way they formed a question.

"Yes, I can see that it might be so," the father gazed toward his son smiling and nodded affirmation.

"Lupita's Quinceanera," Vicente said.

"Yes, it is the tradition. She will become a woman tonight. I am very happy for you, my son."

"Thank you, Father."

Outside their tent, the night air was filling with the sound of music coming from the small plaza in the center of Caldera.

"How do they make such beautiful music with so few instruments?" Vicente mused, not expecting an answer.

Vicente's father placed a hand on his son's shoulder, "It's because the music comes from the musician, not the instrument." The men exchanged a glance and another fragment of information about truth and life was passed from father to son.

The gay music and voices told of happiness and a prosperity measured by some other value than pesos. In this small garden called Caldera, there was a blossom on a plant nourished with this happiness and prosperity. It was a flower with a form, color, scent and promise not seen in any other village of the Hacienda Escobedo. The name of this rose was "Guadalupe".

Vicente threw back the flap of the tent and strode into the magic of the soft night air. He looked up at the stars so big and bright he felt he could reach up and pull one down. He knew this was going to be an enchanted evening.

The Zocalo in the center of the village was decorated with lanterns made with candles surrounded by paper. Everyone was already there, and the fiesta was underway when Vicente and his father arrived. A large fire pit was being refueled, sending sparkling cinders floating across the scene like a few thousand fireflies were flying through. Vicente caught sight of his rosebud kneeling near the fire. As if summoned, she looked up, arose, and she and Vicente walked toward each other. They met in an embrace as dancers and the music of a ranchero began. Locks of Lupe's raven hair were woven into a silver tiara, a black lace shawl trimmed in red ribbons adorned her shoulders and a red silk sash wrapped around her delicate waist. She wore shoes of black leather with wooden heels. They danced.

As if frozen when the ranchero ended, Vicente and Lupe held the center of the dance floor as the others left it. The first few notes came from the guitar and Lupe recognized the music immediately. She pulled a black lace fan from the sash at her waist and with a flick of her wrist it spread wide, hiding her face except for her sparkling eyes. As the flamenco rhythm began Lupe tapped the heels of her shoes on the wooden planks beneath her feet. All the elders who watched the two were aware that they were witnessing a ritual as old as civilization. The men gazed into the never aging eyes in the wrinkled faces of their women and they reminisced of when it was their time to do the dance of life. Vicente began clapping his hands as the pulse of the dance became electric and it seemed the rhythm of the guitar and Lupe were driven by his clapping. Her skirt began lifting and twirling as she went spinning around Vicente. He stiffened his shoulders back and arched his spine, like when he stood up against one of his bulls. Lupe made passes at him while he turned on the soles of his boots in perfect half circles, pointing his index fingers at her. Every person at the fiesta now stood at the edge of the dance pavilion clapping along with the rhythm of the music, someone occasionally shouting an "Ole!" The dance exhausted itself with Lupe reclining in Vicente's arms, her hair dangling, almost touching the floor.

He lifted her and ached to kiss her, although chivalry, her honor, and propriety demanded his restraint. There was not a single heart present, not beating in unison with the two who were destined to live magical lives that only those who love each other can have.

As the onlookers broke into applause, Vicente and Lupe stepped through the crowd and moved away from the music and gaiety. Lupe's pace was quick as she ran through the casitas. She allowed him to catch her and he kissed her, but she quickly broke away. He caught her again and hugged tightly and he kissed her but again she broke away and ran. He chased her until she stopped where two horses were tied. They had halters on and were blanketed. Lupe quickly mounted.

"Where are we going?" Vicente asked.

"You will see. Follow me," Lupe said as she kicked the horse and galloped away.

After riding fast through the moonlit night for ten minutes, they arrived at the rocky face of the mountains against which Caldera was nestled.

"Where are you taking me?" he asked again as she grabbed his hand and led him.

"There's an entrance into the mountain," Lupe said as they approached large boulders. Vicente noticed a soft breeze on his face as if the mountain was exhaling a warm, moist, sweet breath.

"I want to show you a place we call, Los Ollas de Plata." They went hand in hand zigzagging through several boulders. There was a torch and matches at the entrance to a small tunnel. Lupe lit the torch and they entered. After thirty steps, they were inside a cavernous room.

"I hear water," Vicente said, looking toward an echoing sound from within the cavern. It was the sound of water dripping onto the surface of a pool.

"You hear the hot mineral springs. It is a magic place, I brought you to see it." Lupe said with excitement driven by thoughts of what might be this evening.

"During the day, enough light finds its way into here that you can see everything. Come, I'll show you."

Lupe took a step forward and their arms extended between them. Vicente pulled her back to him, embraced her, and kissed her. It was a long, delicious, wet kiss, that fused their souls.

He pushed her back and looked into her eyes, searching deep into her soul, "Lupe, before you answer my question, you must know something. I intend to enlist in the Federales the next chance I get and will likely have to leave for the fighting. Will you marry me?"

"My father must approve first," she answered.

"I have asked your father and he has spoken with mine. They both give us their blessings."

"Yes." The answer can immediately, exquisitely simple, exquisitely complete as his arms enveloped her. He began kissing her.

She allowed the kissing to continue until she was delirious before she pushed him back. "Come mi amore, I must tell my mother and sister."

Lupe led Vicente by the hand, out of the mountain, and they rode to the fiesta with news that sent all the partygoers into a frenzied celebration.

CHAPTER 3

"Isn't this lace exquisite?" Lupe's mother commented.

"Where did you get it?" asked one of the women sitting in the circle.

"I bought it at the central market in the Capitol. It's from Paris," Lupe's mother answered.

"We have put so much silver on this dress, I'm afraid she won't be able to carry it." Lupe's grandmother said with a bit of a pride in her voice. "Why are the sleeves so puffy?" the old woman asked.

"It is fashion, grandma." Juanita told her as she stitched.

"And why does it have a tail? It is going to get dirty."

"No, Grandma, it won't. The girls will walk behind and carry it for her. After the wedding, we will take it off. Lupe's daughter will have it on her wedding dress someday," Juanita said.

"I won't be here to see that, but it will be beautiful." Grandma's eyes became alive with excitement as she saw the vision in her head. "What is Lupe wearing in her hair, la tiara?"

"No. She wants Lupine flowers in her hair." Juanita replied softly, leaning to place her cheek against the wrinkled skin of her grandmother's arm.

"That's what I had when I was a bride. It's so beautiful." Grandma said as tears filled her eyes.

* * * * *

Six unmarried girls of Caldera giggled as they carried the ten-foot train of the dress behind Lupe. Lupe paused between each step as she approached Vicente.

The groom wore a black wool suit, black leather boots, and a black beaver hat. Metal buttons closed the jacket, decorations adorned the sleeves at the cuff and ran down the seams of his trousers. He stood tall alongside his bride as Father Miguel de la Penza gave God's blessing on a union blessed by the fathers of these young people. Young people already recognized as leaders who would guarantee a prosperous future.

"Vicente, will you love this woman?" the padre's voice was loud.

"I will love you," Vicente said, looking into Lupe's eyes.

Turning to face the people assembled, "I will love her for my whole life."

Vicente's Godfather Bernardino Gonzales handed him the band of gold, which he placed on Lupe's slender finger.

"Will you love this man?" The padre asked Lupe.

"I love you, Vicente, I will love you as long as I live," she said.

In a strong, proud voice, Father Miguel announced, "You are a man and his wife. Go on, kiss her my son," happiness radiating from his face.

The final words being said, Vicente kissed Lupe with a kiss that stopped the passing of time. Musicians began playing and a roaring cheer broke out from the guests. Men tossed their hats into the air and began firing their pistols, spitting fire and puffs of smoke, taking care not to shoot a hole in someone's best hat.

Although the music, drinking and dancing would go on until early in the morning, the newlyweds stole away from the fiesta as sunset gave way to darkness.

"Where are we going?"

"I want to go to Los Ollas," Vicente said.

"In my dress?" Lupe blurted out, smiling, excitedly and not really protesting but surprised.

"I will buy you a hundred dresses, mi amore." Vicente said, and a scene from the past repeated itself, except this time Vicente had two horses prepared and waiting. The newlyweds rode to the face of the mountains.

Once inside the cavern, he led her toward the echoing sounds of water. They arrived at the pool of water and as if ordained, the moon was directly over an airshaft. A ray of light was beaming down onto the surface of the pool. Bubbles of gas rose and broke, releasing a sweet smelling, intoxicating vapor that floated and swirled on the surface of the water before drifting into the air.

"The water is always a perfect temperature. We can bathe if you wish." Lupe said as she turned her dress fell to the ground. She was naked and in the water before Vicente could form a thought or voice a word. Once in the water she turned and faced him, her breasts halfway hidden, half exposed. She beckoned to him and he quickly undressed and joined her in the pool. They embraced and began a dance that had no music, no steps, but there was a rhythm of hearts beating as one. Lupe knew she could now give him her feminine gifts. She pressed the rounded female parts of her body firmly against him.

Every physical sensation Vicente's body was capable of he now felt. He made a pallet of their clothes and there on the soft sand alongside warm pools, in Los Ollas de Plata, he and his rose enjoyed the ultimate lovers' pleasure.

* * * * *

When the husband and wife eventually found their way back to where the wedding had taken place, there was a wagon prepared for them. All the cargo was removed, and the linens and quilts of Lupe's dowry lined the bottom. Softly, the moon penetrated the canvas and illuminated the chamber with a warm romantic light, appropriate for the occasion.

After several hours, they fell asleep in each other's arms. Their brief sleep was awakened by the activity of their wagon being hitched to a team of horses. It was the last wagon added to the caravan already formed. The signal was given, and they departed for the Hacienda Escobedo.

Lupe lifted the flap of canvas and gazed out the back of the wagon toward the mountains which stood majestically, guarding her childhood home. A gentle sprinkle of light spring rain was falling, the air was fresh and sweet with the smells she loved. Opaque rays from the rising sun made their way through the billowy clouds and reached down, touching the new blades of grass springing from the soil. The warmth of the light radiated perfume from the sagebrush and the pungent odor of camphor came from the delicate flowers of the Blue Curl. A wave of sadness and longing fueled a brief flash of desire to turn back, but this could not last. Her happiness quickly returned. She crawled through the wagon and climbed into the seat beside her husband.

"My heart will miss Caldera," she said sadly.

"Do not be sad. You can come with me and we will visit here every spring during the roundup, I promise you, mi Rosa." It was the first time she heard the love-name no other ears but hers would ever hear.

"Maybe someday we will return, to live here?"

"Many things are possible," he said as he held the reins in one hand and put his arm around the shoulder of his rose.

CHAPTER 4

New Home, August 28, 1859

T he wagon crested the final peak on the journey through the narrow mountain pass. A large wooden cross stood prominently on the highest peak.

"There it is," Vicente pointed his finger into the valley. In the center were the tiny red roofs. They were contained by the wall that surrounded the Hacienda Escobedo. He handed Lupe a pair of mira lejos. She looked through them into the valley at the hacienda, searching with wonderment and excitement in her soul.

"Our home," she whispered in awe.

"Si, me amour, our home," Vicente agreed as he adjusted the brake on the wagon in preparation for the long steep winding grade ahead.

"How long will it take?"

"About two hours if no one breaks down," he answered.

It was a very long two hours of bumping and jostling as Lupe's hungry eyes consumed every new detail. Finally, their wagon passed through the heavy wooden gates. They were immediately met by the shouts and cheers from joyous men, women and happy children. A dozen barking dogs joined in, to welcome home their masters.

As their wagon broke away from the others, Lupe identified parts of the metropolis. There was Don Escobedo's expansive house, storehouses, many barns, stables, corrals, and dwellings. Her heart raced as her gaze moved from one visual feast to the next. Where would their home be?

The question was answered almost as soon as it was asked. Vicente stopped the wagon in front of a little house with a small porch and a tiled roof. Fresh whitewash reflected the sunlight brilliantly and the little casita seemed to come alive, welcoming Lupe making her ecstatically happy. She did not wait for Vicente to assist her. She jumped down on the ground and ran inside. The walls were finished with plaster and painted white. The floor was made of smooth boards rubbed with sweet smelling bees wax polished to a luster. As she walked on the planks, although they were new acquaintances, they made comforting sounds like the voices of old friends. There were glass paned windows with muslin curtains and sunlight filled the room. A little perfect size table with two thatched seat chairs sat against the wall. The bedroom had a bed, its mattress stuffed with cotton. On it were two feather pillows. She picked up one, buried her face into it and inhaled the sweet unmistakable smell, the smell of comfort.

"Come back out here. Help me unload," Vicente called through the door.

Although happy beyond imagination and consumed with the desire to never leave the perfect home she had just fell in love with, she acquiesced to her husband's request.

Lupe stepped outside onto the small porch. Vicente was hiding beside the door and caught her sweeping her up into his arms.

"We must observe tradition," he said stepping back into the house with her cradled in his arms. "We don't want any bad luck," he said as he kicked the door shut and lovingly tossed his Rosa onto the bed.

Several hours later, when they began to unload their wagon, the people who lived in the neighboring houses came out and helped. They also brought with them welcome gifts of food and items of utility.

As the day ended, the newlyweds stood on the porch of their new home soaking in the colors of the sun as it settled down behind the mountains to the west.

"We have morning sun, evening shade and this beautiful sunset, mi amour. I love this little house and I love you." Lupe said. They kissed.

Vicente again swept her up off her feet and carried her inside to their bed.

CHAPTER 5

Pica Diablo

Lupe placed the stack of fresh towels on the shelf in the closet and stepped outside onto the porch. The air was ripe with the smell of the barn cart that passed by, carrying the morning harvest from the stalls to be spread in the gardens.

She found her husband in the round corral, working with a mare and its foal, a stallion, black as midnight without a single marking. The colt immediately lost interest in chasing his mother and walked over to the fence. Lupe extended her hand and the colt sniffed her fingers, whinnied, and kicked up his heels as he ran back to his mother's side.

"Come in," Vicente called over to her.

The mare had a long rope attached to her halter. Lupe stood in the center of the pen with her husband as he swung his end of the rope in the direction of the mare. The horse broke into a trot, the colt joined her and circling at her tail.

Vicente whistled and clicked his tongue against the roof of his mouth and the mare began to gallop.

The little horse, at five days old, could run with his mother.

The horses ran the circumference of the pen several times.

"That's enough," Vicente called. The mare stopped and turned, walking to where the two stood stood. Vicente took hold of her halter as Lupe petted the mare's face.

"She is very beautiful. Ouch! Dios Mio!" Lupe cried out as she jumped away, turning to look at the little horse that had bitten her on the buttock.

"Diablo!" She shouted in the colt's face. The little horse took two steps backward, startled by the force of her voice.

"He has a lot of guts," Vicente said as he made a lasso and tossed it around the little colt's neck.

"He's going to be one of the best we've ever had," Vicente said.

"Can he be my horse?" Lupe asked.

"That is not for me to say. He is the property of the Don and even if you succeeded in getting his permission, it would again be necessary to get the final, more difficult permission."

"What do you mean?" Lupe asked.

"He must permit it," Vicente said motioning toward the colt at the end of the rope.

Lupe looked toward the little stallion that was watching her intently. "You're going to be my horse. Do you hear me, Pica Diablo?"

The little horse flared his nostrils, reared up on his hind legs and kicked his front feet in the air.

* * * * *

Lupe walked into the barn, her boots dusty, her face covered with beads of sweat and began brushing the three-year-old, Diablo standing in his stall.

"You must have ridden far today. He's been here forty-five minutes. I took your saddle off." Bernardo's words communicated his amusement. "I'm not sure which of you two is the master and which one is the servant," Bernardo laughed.

"Make no mistake. He will be my horse," Lupe said as Diablo craned his neck back looking at her and farted.

The next day, like almost every day, Lupe saddled Diablo around ten in the morning and rode out the gate. Today she headed for the arroyo three miles south of the rancho. When they arrived, she tied a close hobble on Diablo's front ankles and allowed him to graze on the grass that grew around an old quarry pond. It was her plan to swim, as she often did; however, when she jumped down onto the flat rock near the water's edge, she heard a loud popping sound and saw a bone protruding through the skin between her knee and ankle.

How can this not hurt? She asked herself before concluding that in time it was going to hurt terribly.

Diablo immediately appeared on the ledge above and although hobbled, jumped down nimbly onto the flat rock, landing gingerly so as not to touch Lupe. He lowered his nose and kissed the top of her head.

She untied his hobble.

"Help me, Diablo. Go get Vicente."

Without hesitation, the stallion jumped back up onto the ledge and galloped away.

Only thirty minutes passed before she heard voices echoing off the walls of the quarry. Diablo's face was the first to look down on her followed by Vicente's and Bernardo's.

Vicente applied a temporary splint on the broken bone, and they made a travel sled, attaching it to Diablo's saddle.

The next day, the bone had been set and Lupe was resting well. Bernardo told her for the first time a story that would be repeated, embellished, and repeated many times.

"When he galloped across the yard into the barn, I thought he had run away from you, as usual, and I started laughing. Only, when I tried to remove the saddle, he spun around and kicked a hole in the wall. Then he reared, struck his feet at me, and ran out of the barn, bucking like he had gone completely loco. He then ran back into the barn, crying out as if he were in great pain. Vicente came in, grabbed him by his bridle and tried to calm him but he dragged Vicente out of the barn toward the main gate.

I said, "Lupe must be in trouble," so we saddled our horses and Diablo led us straight to you, mejia, without ever breaking a stride. Something tells me he is going to be your horse from now on."

The story varied slightly, depending on the teller. In Vicente's version, he is the one who said, 'Lupe must be in trouble.'

Bernardo's hunch proved to be dead on. Never again did the horse do anything other than Lupe's will. She began having a love affair. It was between the beautiful senora and the big beautiful black stallion.

CHAPTER 6

Friends and Enemies

"Fry it till it's crunchy. Gringos like it almost burnt," Lupe said to Juana, dropping two pounds of bacon on the table near the stove. Juana had come to the Hacienda when Lupe was about to give birth to her second child and stayed to live there.

"And make one-half the tortillas with flour. There are six of them. Don't forget they want boiled coffee."

"I have it already. How can they stand to drink that nasty stuff?"

"I don't know, but in the morning, they like it as much as Carmen likes my milk," Lupe said as she gently squeezed the cheek of the baby whose beautiful eyes followed each movement in the kitchen from her bassinet.

Diego entered the kitchen and placed water pots on the fires.

"Are you sure everyone has towels?" Lupe asked her son.

"Yes. I'm eight, mother. You don't have to tell me everything," he said, annoyed that he should be questioned about such a thing.

"Well, I'm sure you know then, we need three chickens for the dinner tonight."

"Yes, mother," Diego nodded as he passed out the door.

"And you know to get all those pinfeathers out this time."

"Yes, mother."

"Why do they come so late in the night?" Juana asked.

"They come and go in the night, thinking they will not be seen. Everything is a secret these days. They think spying eyes are everywhere."

"They are calling for the coffee, Lupe. Take it."

"They'll get it soon enough."

"Even though they just get out of bed, they need the coffee to make them relax. I don't understand it," Juana said, shaking her head. "Are they the blue ones or the gray ones?"

"Gringos are gringos," Lupe said as she readied the tray with the coffee service and left for the dining room where Don Escobedo, Vicente, and his father sat at one side of the large table. Across from them sat three soldiers in blue uniforms.

The man who was speaking with Don Escobedo quieted and his eyes fixed on Lupe.

"Speak freely in my house, Major. Everyone in it I have known from their birth."

"We need three hundred head. Can you do that?" the officer asked.

"So many," Don Escobedo raised his eyebrows.

"We have an army to feed, sir," the American explained.

"Everyone has an army to feed. Even so, yes, we can do that."

The Captain at the Major's side spoke, "Do you have horses?"

Don Escobedo looked to Vicente's father, who provided the answer.

"We can supply you forty, saddle broke, three years old."

"Good, very good," the Major said. "We will buy those."

A Mexican man, medium in height and build, dressed in Charro clothes, entered the dining room. Don Escobedo rose as did Vicente and his father. The Americans followed suit.

"Gentlemen, may I present to you, General Porfirio Diaz, of the Republican Army of Mexico."

Extending his hand, in hospitality General Diaz said, "Welcome to Mexico, gentlemen," and joined his countrymen seated at the table.

"And what do you propose to pay for three hundred beef and forty good Mexican horses, senor?" General Diaz asked.

The Colonel motioned to the Lieutenant, who sat with him and the Major. The young man excused himself and returned with a new Springfield Model

1861 musket with a bayonet affixed. He handed the weapon to General Diaz and laid upon the table in front of him a dozen paper loads, each containing a black powder charge, a .58 caliber conical mini-ball, and a percussion cap. The ammunition package was the latest technology in loading and allowed the musketeer to fire twice in quick succession.

"We propose to pay with one hundred cases of rifles with bayonets and ten thousand loads of ammunition. I believe these weapons are more valuable to you than gold, are they not, senor?"

"Yes, they are, but these animals you desire are also desired by many. The price will be one hundred and ten cases of rifles and fifteen thousand packages of ammunition.

The Colonel and Captain leaned together, whispering back and forth.

"We can do business, gentlemen."

"We can have the animals ready for you in three days."

"Excellent, excellent." The American was very happy.

"If you will excuse me, gentlemen," General Diaz stood, picking up the loads from the table and, with the new rifle in hand, exited the room.

The Union Army officer asked, "Have the Confederates been here?"

"Senor, you know the price of my freedom and the security of my home, are dependent upon being cordial to all who come here, including the two colors of the Americans, the Germans, French, and my own countrymen of differing views. They all must leave with something of value. In these days everyone who visits has an army to supply or cause to feed and they are willing to pay a fair price for what they want. Except the French bastards. When they visit my home, they bring wagons heavy with troops and guns, their purses light with money. They insinuate how lucky I am, lucky that Maxmillian does not take what he needs, rather than buying it at any price. As for you, sir, you are a gentleman, and you are welcome in my home at any time."

"We will soon be at the end of our war and I am sure that when it is over our country will come to your aid, sir. The French have supplied and aided our enemy. General Grant will first put our house in order, and will help Benito Juarez rid your country of the French occupiers and put Mexico's house back in order, sir."

The distinct sound of a Springfield musket popped, sending a slight concussion through the air, startling Lupe as she entered the dining room from the kitchen with bacon, tortillas and eggs for the hungry men.

The business being concluded at an early hour gave the Americans and Mexicans time to visit one another. For the balance of this day, the time was occupied with pleasant activities. Discourse soared as they conversed regarding philosophy, exchanging knowledge from their perspectives about topics of the day. They shared congeniality and hospitality of a quality and character known only to those of high rank, privilege, and position.

Lupe was kept busy seeing to their every need and making sure their visit was pleasant. She had occasion to wait upon all who visited Hacienda Escobedo. Many of these visitors had become her friends. She was indeed a warm, charming, and bright intellect and, having been privileged to overhear or share in all of conversations taking place in the household, was very well informed. Through this exposure, she had become quite polished in her language and demeanor.

Diego, who spoke fluent English and French, was somewhat of a mascot for those who enjoyed the hospitality of the household. He reminded these gentlemen and ladies that posterity had promise, youthful intelligence and exuberance were alive and well in the desolation of the harsh landscapes that made up most of Mexico.

CHAPTER 7

An Army of Peasants

Don Escobedo knew the balance was tipping in favor of victory and that it was time to declare what had always been his allegiance to the Republic of Mexico. He summoned all the hacienda's caballeros with orders to bring all things that would have value going into battle. During the two weeks that followed, each day saw new arrivals of men and women on foot, carrying their meager possessions with them. Horsemen, wagons and carts loaded with women and children, arms and goods necessary to provide for an army.

Lupe and Juana were put in charge of gathering provisions from the rancho, loading and organizing the wagons. Special attention was given to making bandages and packaging them so they would remain dry and clean. General Escobedo gave into Lupe's charge the field surgery kit, filled with cruel looking tools and instruments which would be used more than anyone cared to think about at the time.

Half of the muskets and ammunition from the sale of Escobedo cattle and horses was taken by General Diaz but the balance became the property of Don Escobedo. The most able-bodied men were given new rifles. They took practice shooting at targets and reloading. They lunged at straw scarecrows with the sharp steel skewers attached to the muzzles of their weapons. General Escobedo's army, though poor and uneducated was well armed, well trained, and ready for the fight to rid their country of Maximillian, the French invaders, and occupiers.

A courier arrived with a dispatch from General Diaz giving marching orders for Escobedo's army, outlining their mission. They were to engage and hold a contingent of nine hundred regular French Marines encamped near the town of Pueblo.

When the army prepared to move out, there were one thousand soldiers, many of whom had their wives with them, who refused to stay behind. By necessity, they were taking their children with them in the wagons and carts. Many of the soldiers were on foot, choosing to march and allowing their families to ride.

As the procession rolled through the pass in the hills above the Hacienda, Lupe looked back on her home wondering if she would ever return.

CHAPTER 8

Gun Powder, Chili Powder, Blood and Lead

nother three minutes passed in slumber as Lupe snuggled against Vicente's warm body. One hundred and eighty glorious seconds filled with the scent of sagebrush, her mouth dreaming of her mother's mole, a warm expectation of the sun's radiant heat, and the desire for her husband's fingers to play secret music on her physical heartstrings. Another three minutes when life was normal, life was good. Carmen whimpering could not interrupt this bliss. From twenty feet behind her one of the wounded expelled a low pitched, painful moan. Lupe knew his suffering would come to an end today. She and Juana would dig his grave along with the dozens of others in the ravine. Those killed outright were the lucky ones, she thought. This thought began to remove the mystical quilt provided by her dreams. She opened her eyes. Another day had begun.

Sliding out the side of the serape without disturbing Vicente, she placed wood onto the glowing coals of last night's fire. As if choreographed, the other women rose and began the quiet dance of preparing the morning meal. The glow of thirty fires spread across the mesa and began to flicker in the softness of the predawn light. There were nine hundred and seventy-eight able-bodied men and forty-two wounded, one hundred and thirty-six women with two hundred and twenty- three children to feed. No less important were the seventy horses, twenty burros, nine mules, six cows, numerous dogs, and flocks of chickens. These numbers were important to her and each morning she tallied and recounted. General Don Escobedo would inquire.

Each evening the amber glow of dusk brought dirty, exhausted men back to the camp. The officers who led the men fighting skirmishes and battles would huddle in General Escobedo's tent. Lupe's ears and eyes were as busy as her delicate fingers as she nourished these heroes with scraps of meat, tortillas, and hominy. After the men finished the telling all critical details, she would pour them a small glass of mescal to erase from their tortured minds the memory of the day's brutality.

At seven a.m. every morning, the scene would be repeated, except that the men who gathered in the tent were cleaner, their eyes telling of refreshed spirits, ready to hear their leader's words of inspiration, direction and purpose. They would leave the tent each morning renewed and enlivened by the precious hours passed in the camp.

Lupe brought cool water and refreshment to all who visited the big tent and was present to listen carefully to all dispatches, reports, commands and discussions regarding enemy strength, strategy, tactics, re-supply, and progress of the fighting. What General Escobedo knew; Lupe also knew. He would inquire of her daily regarding the food stocks, the condition of each wounded man, and the mood of the camp. He was keenly aware that the beat of the camp was the beat of the heart and soul of his army. At the camp was the essence of what the men fought for.

CHAPTER 9

The Cannons Roar

"Be safe, my brave warrior," Lupe called as Vicente waved back. He rode away on Diablo toward the fighting like he did every day, but today would soon prove to be exceptionally unordinary. After the women had the morning chores attended to and were beginning the mid-day routine, the air recoiled with thunderous concussions from French cannons. Every person in the camp froze, their eyes looked from one to another in horror. The French had introduced artillery into the fight. They knew that cannonballs threw shrapnel when they exploded, maiming more men than they killed. Lupe thought about bandages and tequila as she drew a deep breath. For a moment, she allowed herself to feel a deep sorrow, sorrow that would have no place in her mind when wounded men were presented for surgery. This sorrow seemed the antithesis of bravery.

A tiny raindrop fell softly upon Lupe's cheek and she looked skyward and prayed that it was not a wayward promise, but it would become a deluge. Within a few minutes, the sounds of booming cannon were replaced with booming thunder and she knew the fighting had ended for the day.

Soon the men began returning carrying dead and wounded, many were bleeding badly. Lupe and Juana began triage and soon Lupe's clothing and hands were covered in blood. She looked up from her duty more frequently; she had not yet seen Vicente nor Don Escobedo. A sick, panicky feeling was forming in her stomach as fewer men were unaccounted for. Then the sight came that caused her knees to buckle to the ground and her hands to cover her face. Bernardo was leading Diablo, his mane and empty saddle covered in congealed blood. For a moment she was tempted to give in to her emotions, sink into mourning, but her duty raised her to her feet. The men and women needed her. They needed each other to hold together.

When the most difficult cases were attended to, Lupe sat down near her wagon and allowed herself to sob. Juana brought her a plate of food.

"Hermana, you must eat something."

"I have no stomach for it."

"You must eat.

Bernardo approached and kneeled, "I saw the General shot and fall from his horse. I tried to get to him, but it was impossible. We tried our best but had to leave some behind."

"Do you think he was killed?" Juana asked.

"Did you see Vicente?" Lupe asked.

"No, mejia. I do not know. The French know the butchery Medina and Diaz are doing to their prisoners. I suspect the French are doing the same, killing everyone."

"Vicente," Lupe sobbed.

"I think we have met a bad end. We can go into the field tomorrow, but it won't be us who return. The French will return here to our camp," Bernardo said.

Lupe stiffened, "We cannot allow that to happen. Bring the officers to the big tent in twenty minutes. I have an idea."

"Si, Senora."

CHAPTER 10

Brothers and Sisters of Arms

"I go this way." Lupe moved her delicate finger across the map. "Twelve men will go with me. Juana will go with everyone else, advance staying on the back side of this hill. Give the animals corn every ten minutes, they must be kept silent. Tie everything down tightly, if something jingles, rattles or the animals make noise, you might be found out and we lose our advantage. If we lose our advantage, we lose everything." Lupe eyed them carefully, making sure each one understood the importance of the element of surprise. You will attack their flank from here," she tapped her finger on the map and then pointed to the distance where the rising moon gave definition to the hills. "You should seek high ground. See how their fires stop here?" She pointed to the glow in the distance, marking their fires and then back to the map, again tapping her finger to illustrate where the edge of their camp was.

"They will have pickets, just like we do. Martine, go ahead of everyone, use the chivota. Cut their throats. Make sure they do not sound the alarm.

"Si Lupe, I understand," Martine responded solemnly.

"You must wait until the last moment of darkness before you begin to fire. Everyone will attack; no one will fall back. We will not keep a reserve. You must be in position before the sun rises. Everything depends on it."

"We risk all," Armando stated bluntly.

"The time has come for it. We are ready. We will surprise them and defeat them."

Armando said, "Lupe, it is a long way, a lot of hard walking. We will be tired from our lack of sleep."

"You speak the truth. We are tired and, in the morning, you will be hungry, but I promise you, when the fighting starts, you will be filled with energy and courage."

"We can do it," Armando concluded.

"Every Frenchman with any fight in him will advance to the front when you attack. When you have them fully engaged, I will move swiftly on the other flank where they have their command post."

"Lupe, what do we do with our little ones and the wounded?"

"The little ones and the wounded will be here when we return."

Lupe stood and looked across the small valley that separated her camp from the French. The sound of their squeezebox and violin stopped and was replaced by the clanking of equipment.

"Tonight, the French think their victory will take place tomorrow in the valley, after they have slept well, eaten plenty of hot food and are prepared for the field. Tomorrow, the fight will take place in their camp, while sleep is in their eyes, their bellies are empty, and they are in nothing but their underwear."

* * * * *

Juana laid her hand gently upon Lupe's shoulder. "It's time. Here," Juana put two warm tortillas in Lupe's hand. "I must go now and catch up with Bernardo. Take care, my sister. I will see you when it is finished." Juana mounted and rode away.

"Momma," came out of the darkness and Diego came, leading Carmen by the hand. "Where has everyone gone?"

"Don't worry, my brave man, they will return soon enough. Will you do something for me?"

"Sure, Momma, what is it?"

"I am going to help the others and while I am gone, will you look after the camp for me? You know what to do."

"Of course, I will," the young Diego said firmly.

"Good, my son," Lupe said as she comforted her darling little Carmen, who had her fingers tightly clasped to her mother's skirt.

"Don't be afraid, I will return soon, but I must go now." With a muster of courage, she turned away from her children.

"We must be swift and quiet," she said to the twelve selected to go with her. The party moved into the soft darkness of the sky, lit only by a sliver of moon.

She looked back at Diego outlined by the fire, watching them leave. At nine years old he was already a veteran and veterans knew any soldier leaving the camp might not return. Although he wouldn't show it, Lupe sensed a pained look on his face as he turned and picked up his sister. He was the leader of the camp now and she knew he would do well; he always did. Thoughts of their lives together quickly flashed through her consciousness from the sweet day of his birth and exploded into the realization that this might be the last glimpse she ever saw of him. The experience ended when her thoughts returned to the present and she faced back to the path her comrades were on. She knew their plan had a good chance of success, and success was her guarantee that she would return to her children. This thought brought the first of many bursts of adrenalin that would energize her body and sedate her mind through the coming hours.

CHAPTER 11

The Surrender

There was no reason for Lupe to tell them the latest intelligence about the number of French troops they were attacking. The only thing certain about the strength and position of the enemy was that it's always uncertain, subject to the omission, exaggeration, and interpretation of the witness. Even so, she expected them to be outnumbered five to one. The element of surprise would hopefully even the odds.

Lupe and her dozen traveled quickly and quietly through the night for many hours. As if the muskets firing in the distance was the cause, the uncertainty of the landscape clouded in darkness became illuminated. The fear experienced by a soldier not yet engaged in combat, disappeared.

A jolt of adrenalin rushed over Lupe. She sensed anguish and suffering; people were dying. Many would die this morning, her soldiers, her friends and loved ones. Some French would die, some without the honor of being killed in combat, killed without a weapon in their hand, shot in the back without even a trouser or a tunic covering their underwear. Regardless of how it was done, the enemy must be killed, incapacitated, or captured.

A full minute passed before the sound of the French bugle was heard. The army of professionals had been awakened from sleep, surprised by the army of peasants. Another minute passed before the pattern of fire changed from the sound of Mexicans firing rapidly, shooting the unarmed, the panicking, disoriented, to the sound of volleys being exchanged by attackers and defenders.

Lupe and her party arrived at a spot where they overlooked the adobe which reported to be the command post. There was a French flag flying upon a tall pole attached to the building. At the front, a bugler was blowing commands, rhythms of sounds the troops were trained to understand. As she predicted, there was no rear guard. Litter carriers were bringing the wounded away from the fighting, taking place three hundred yards away. The command post had been converted into a field hospital.

Lupe and her dozen crept out a clump of trees fifty yards away from the enemy and they yelled, "Viva Mexico!" as they advanced, shooting several litter carriers who laid down their cargo, un-slung their muskets and prepared to fire. Others dropped their stretchers and ran. Only minutes passed before a broom draped with a white towel bearing evidence of fresh blood protruded through a window.

"We are coming in," Lupe announced.

"Enter." The response came from inside.

Lupe stepped through the wooden door to see a severely wounded officer lying on the table being attended to by a surgeon, who himself had a serious wound in the right bicep, his arm hanging limp at his side.

"We must have your weapons, gentlemen," Lupe said.

The French handed over their weapons. The wounded man on the table winced with pain as he held up his hand holding a gold-handled saber, encased in a silver scabbard, bearing many inscriptions and insignias describing its legacy. The elder man spoke.

"I am Colonel Jacques de Vallier. I presume you are here to announce your victory. I surrender to you, Madame, conditional upon your promise to grant mercy and quarter to my men."

"You have my promise, senor."

Lupe accepted the sword. She saw an anguished look upon the distinguished face, a look telling of a hurt far greater than pain caused by wounds, a pain burning not into the flesh, but into the soul.

"Bugler; signal surrender," the commandant ordered.

The horn began to blow, its music heard only between the thunder of gunfire, which became sporadic and was replaced altogether by the crying and occasional screams coming from those who were affected by the horrors of the past half hour. These cries of pain and suffering were coming from her people as well as from the French, but these disturbing sounds were better in comparison to the sound of musket fire.

"Get my bag. Bring all the wounded here," Lupe instructed one of her men. Over the past months. she had removed hundreds of musket balls and pieces of shrapnel, stitched up lacerations. and even amputated shattered limbs. She was as qualified as any army surgeon.

"Can you use my help?" she asked the French doctor.

"Yes, I am Jean Pierre Farre'. I'm afraid I've lost the use of my favorite hand, and a steady hand is very much needed here. The bullet is dreadfully close to his heart."

Lupe leaned over the officer lying on the table and saw they had already undone his tunic and cut open his blouse to expose the hole in his chest.

Juana entered the surgery with the medical kit, setting it down and unrolling it to expose instruments encased in small pockets stitched onto the canvas backing. She stepped to the other side of the table next to the French doctor, ready to assist in the operation.

"Do you have whiskey?" Lupe inquired.

"Yes," the handsome doctor answered and stepped to a trunk, removed a bottle of cognac, handing it to Lupe.

"Here, drink as much of this as you can," she uncorked the bottle and handed it to the wounded Colonel who took it, tipped it up, and swallowed several large gulps.

"Drink more," she instructed, and he returned the bottle to his lips and swallowed more of the elixir.

"I need light."

A lamp was placed on the table near the roll of tools. Lupe turned the wick up, so the light was as bright as possible. She removed a wooden stick from the end pocket of the tool roll and placed it into the mouth of her patient. She took out a razor from the kit and delicately shaved the hair from around the entrance of the wound. She took up forceps, removed the chimney from the lamp and moved the jaws of the steel pliers back and forth through the flame. She poured cognac into a glass and dipped the forceps into it, then began probing, burrowing into the wound, carefully exploring for the feel of the lead ball. Skill and luck were required not to tear or puncture the vein and arteries attached to the large muscle surrounding it. Lupe pulled the tool out of the wound. In its jaws was the life-threatening musket ball.

Juana, who could easily have been mistaken for a man, took off her sombrero and shook out her raven hair. She removed the heavy bandoleers of bullets crisscrossing her chest and laid aside the equipment of warfare exposing the equipment of womanhood. She withdrew her chivota and sliced open the sleeve of the doctor's shirt.

"It's nothing, it can wait," he said as Juana pulled a handkerchief from her breast pocket, a handkerchief miraculously white and clean, amid the mud and blood. She used it to cleanse the wound in Jean Pierre's arm.

"The bullet has gone through, clean. It will heal well if it doesn't become infected," she said as she smiled the first smile that had been on her lips for many months.

"Thank you," he returned the smile.

"Juana, will you close?" Lupe said as she stepped away from the table and went to find the next person requiring surgical help.

Juana returned to task. She withdrew a needle and sutured the wound.

"You are very skilled, Senora," the doctor complimented.

"Senorita." Juana flashed a brief glance and again a smile came upon her face.

Juana removed the wooden biting stick from the patient's mouth. He said, "Thank you, Madame. I shall be in your debt."

"You need not indenture yourself; it is my honor and a duty. I am sure you would have done the same for me."

"Might I inquire as to your name?"

"Juanita Hidalgo," the response.

"And the other woman, who is she?"

"Guadalupe Hidalgo Martinez. She is my sister."

"Juana Hidalgo, Guadalupe Hidalgo Martinez," as if the utterance of the names had some anesthetic quality, after the Colonel spoke them, his face relaxed and a peace came upon it as he slipped into a coma.

CHAPTER 12

Mercy and Quarter

After Lupe finished the last case that required surgery, she walked around, being sure she looked at the face of every person and every dead body. None was Vicente or Don Escobedo.

Bernardo approached her with bad news. "Lupe, Medina is coming. I just received word. He's coming to rescue us."

"How much time do we have?"

"Not much. They are riding hard because they think we might lose everything today.

"Get Juana, we haven't much time. We have to move fast."

"Si, senora."

Medina's reputation was widespread. He executed all prisoners, sparing none, often taking sport in the methods he used to dispatch them, making sure that if they were not going to hell, for sure they would die hellish deaths.

* * * * *

59

"Martine, you must remove the uniforms from the French dead, down to their long underwear, and put those uniforms on our dead. Make a pile of the bodies where the road crossed the bridge. Put our people on the bottom. I know this will be difficult for you, but you must shoot a hole in the forehead of those dead Frenchmen who will be on top of the pile. It must look like they were executed. Do you understand?"

"Yes, Lupe."

"Okay, go now!"

"Bernardo, bring all the arms, munitions, and provisions together. Divide everything in half. Stack half neatly where Medina can easily load it onto his wagons. Take the other half, the prisoners and all the wounded to Caldera. Avoid all towns and be sure the French stay out of sight. I will come there as soon as I can.

"It is done, mi General," Bernardo said as he stood straight, saluted and turned to leave.

"In the name of the Blessed Virgin, Bernardo, don't start something," Lupe quipped.

Bernardo turned back and gave another salute, "Si, mi General." It was impossible to know how, on such a solemn occasion there was a brief laugh as Bernardo left to do the task he had been assigned.

Lupe found her sister and Jean Pierre attending to the wounded.

"Juana, will you take Diego and Carmen with you and Bernardo. You are going to Caldera with the prisoners and the wounded. Take most of the food and all the medicines and bandages."

"When will you come?"

"I don't know for sure. I need to deal with Medina. He will have ideas for what's left of our army. But know for sure, I will be there as quickly as it is possible."

"Do not worry about the children. I will keep them safe."

"I know you will. God speed sister. I love you."

* * * * *

Upon his arrival, Medina was ecstatic. As Lupe suspected, he quickly set about loading up the supplies and captured arms that had been staged for him.

"We killed them all, according to your standing order. I hope that meets with your approval, General Medina," Lupe stoically reported.

"Good job, good job. Did you say your name was, Guadalupe?"

"Yes, my General. Guadalupe Hidalgo Martinez."

"You are the leader of these soldiers?"

"Yes, soldiers and soldadas. Our General was killed yesterday. Of course, you will appoint someone to lead us," Lupe replied.

"Yes, I see, soldadas," Medina gave her a sideways look.

"I must leave immediately to meet up with General Diaz. We will begin the final march to reclaim our capital. An officer from my staff will take command of the troops here. You will be finished here in a day and then deploy with me. I predict that this will all be over in a weeks' time."

CHAPTER 13

Jean Pierre and Juanita

Shadows danced on the walls of the cavern as the flames of the dying campfire rose for the last time. Juana felt agony in the moaning of Jean Pierre until she could no longer stand the sympathy pains she felt inside her own body. Quietly, she crept to where he slept and lifted back the serape. She lay alongside his shivering, sweating body. She slid out of her clothes and pressed the warmth of her flesh against him.

With a violent jerking motion his eyes opened, and he attempted to get up. Gripping him tightly, Juana held him down.

"It's okay, everything is okay," she murmured, and he relaxed, not because of her words, but because he absorbed the soothing quality of her voice and understood the language of her body.

"Merci," he said, looking into her eyes.

She placed a light kiss on his forehead. He pulled her to him and began a long, deep kiss of passion. The kind of kiss that makes a man feel that his craving for one of life's greatest gifts has been satisfied. A kiss that signaled a complete yielding of a female to a male. She surrendered to him. She was his if he wanted her. Now two people who had encountered each other on the field of battle as enemies, engaged each other as man and woman in an act of love.

* * * * *

Opening her eyes, it took a few moments searching her thoughts before Juana knew where she was. Swimming in her mind were memories of the events of the previous evening. She had spent the whole of her life happily living in the shadow of her older sister. This morning, however, she felt something completely new, as if she had emerged from a chrysalis. She no longer felt like she was just Lupe's little sister. Her mind felt new strength, energy and thought. She felt she had become a woman onto herself and was standing on a stage by herself without her sister. Her life was entirely her own. She gazed up and saw Jean Pierre coming toward her.

"Good morning, Cheri."

"Good morning," she replied as he knelt and kissed her.

"I don't know what's come over me. I have so many things to do," she said and started to get up.

"Rest, my darling, all is well," he said, pushing her back down onto the pallet on the soft sand.

Although a vast departure from her routine, she somehow felt comfortable this morning, allowing the burden for all around her to be borne by the others. A new chapter in her life was beginning, a chapter that had a co-author, and he was there with her holding her hand, looking deeply into her eyes.

She laid her head back onto the pillow and allowed waves of euphoric sensation to surge and ebb as she returned to a dream which danced in her head to the beat of the events that had taken place hours earlier under her serape. For the first time in many years, she was at peace.

CHAPTER 14

The Prison

The large metal doors swung open, screaming out for grease, but the screeches were barely audible above the shouts and yelling of the men held behind them. They had been made aware of the liberation of the city and their impending release. The guards had discarded their French uniforms and left their posts as Diaz and his army approached the city.

Although the jailers had not mistreated the men in their charge, they were reluctant to release them, fearing some might seek retribution or arrest them for aiding and abetting Maximilian.

As the bars of the cell doors swung open, freeing the men, they celebrated. Lupe was jubilant as she aided in freeing them, but her happiness was flawed by a vacancy in her heart, a vacancy that only one possible occupant could ever fill. Suddenly, the sound of his voice entered her mind. "Lupe! Lupe! Lupe!" the sound becoming stronger, louder and more forceful with each repetition until she was compelled to search for a source and, turning, she saw Vicente standing in the cell across the corridor, gripping the bars which separated them. Her hero was alive and well.

Throughout the city there were celebrations. Each had the same gay, festive atmosphere. The only souls not in the same mood were the French and their conspirators, who were locked up and assuredly would face a firing squad within the next few days.

Lupe and Vicente were invited to the grandest of all the parties Mexico City had to offer and there were many. They were also guests at the celebration hosted by Benito Juarez and General Diaz and a cadre of officers who would form the new government. They sat at the table of their patron, General Escobedo.

"It hurts like the devil," Don Escobedo said as he rubbed the bandage just above the knee. "The bullet went in and lodged next to the bone and occasionally, the darn thing hurts all the way up and down my leg. These crutches don't make matters any easier. I feel like a darned fool hobbling around on them."

"Things could be a lot worse. You could be dead," Lupe said. "We were horrified that day when Diablo returned from the battlefield without you and Vicente."

"I must admit those French were very decent. I expected to be shot on the spot, but instead they sent us off to the capital immediately," Vicente said.

"Yes. But not before they gave medical attention to all who needed it. Had it not been for the young surgeon, Farre', I think his name was, he triaged me ahead of his own countrymen and removed the bullet, I would have surely lost my leg, if not my life. The officers were fine fellows, real gentlemen. I wish things could have turned out differently for them. Medina," he said looking around to see who were at the tables nearby, "is such a butcher."

"Just following orders, he would say." Vicente said, not really defending General Medina, but trying to make some sense of the massacre of so many who were captured and executed.

"Some orders must not be obeyed. Dehumanizing the prisoners of war is one of them. It just isn't done," General Escobedo was adamant.

Lupe and Vicente squeezed hands under the table. She had told him about the survivors, including Farre' and Colonel de Vallier, hiding at Caldera, and her plan to help them escape to Texas. From there they had a chance of making it back to their homeland.

"God will have to sort things out. We did what we could. Thank you, Guadalupe for what you did for our people," the General said.

"I did nothing except what had to be done. You must give recognition to everyone when you return to the rancho. When the hour came for them to be strong and brave, they were magnificent."

"Yes, they will all be rewarded, as will you, my daughter."

It was the first, but not the last time that she would hear Senor Escobedo refer to her as family. Lupe's action, taking command of his army and defeating his adversary, saved all that he held near and dear, and although she had earned her way into his heart many years before, he now considered her as close as any of his own blood.

"Vicente, will you stay here with me for a few days? We are setting about the tedious business of establishing a new government and you would be a great assistance to me and the other delegates."

Vicente looked at Lupe for her reaction.

"If you wish. I can leave men here and go with our people back to the Hacienda, put things in order while you put our beloved Mexico back into proper order. When you have completed the task, you come home. We will be ready to begin living again."

"Splendid," the General said, raising his glass of wine as he returned his attention to the gaiety of the dining, dancing, and music.

CHAPTER 15

Rabble Robbers

After helping the returning army settle back into some resemblance of normalcy at the Hacienda Escobedo, Lupe rode on to Caldera. On the way, passing through a narrow place created by rock outcroppings, a dozen men dressed in a hodgepodge of federal army uniforms jumped from behind the rocks and brush. Lupe stopped, assuming they were conducting a routine check for escaping French soldiers. One of the men grabbed Diablo's bridle. The big black stallion was alert and ready for his mistress's spurs but when they did not come, he paused, staying alert.

The professional demeanor of the men lasted only as long as it took for them to realize she was a female in vaqueros clothing. A man with stripes on his sleeve sidled up next to Lupe's leg and placed his hand on her boot.

"Get down, senorita," the man commanded.

"I have a letter signed by General Diaz that authorizes me to travel freely and not be subject to any search or seizure. Furthermore, I will not mention this to General Escobedo who is now waiting, wondering where I am. You have no business with me. Nor I, you."

"General Diaz! Well, the most powerful man in all of Mexico, a man who is seven day's ride from here, celebrating victory in Mexico City, with wine and good food, while we are left out here with nothing, he is your protector. And General Escobedo, do you mean the man who now walks with crutches, who walks on these crutches in Mexico City, the Mariano Escobedo who was shot by the French, the man who cried like a little girl for mercy, is that the Escobedo you are talking about, senorita?"

The men in the little company of soldiers-turned-bandits and worse, began laughing, mocking her with every chant of Escobedo and Diaz's name.

"No, senor. The General Escobedo who is awaiting me is the brave, victorious General Escobedo who will send a company of soldiers to hunt you down like dogs if you do not allow us to pass safely."

"Us? I do not see any, us. I just see you all alone, pretty one."

"You are a man who has little sight and less sense if you think I am alone."

"Senorita, enough of this talk about letters, protectors and companions, get down from your horse."

"You men are not fit to wear the uniforms of soldiers!"

"Who cares what you think, pretty one, we have you here now."

"And your horse," said the man holding Diablo's bridle.

Diablo's head tossed slightly. His ears stood up straight. His eyes opened wide and his nostrils flared and snorted. He was aware there were games afoot and sensed he would have a part to play in it.

Lupe pulled a pistol from the waistband of her trousers, a gun that had been concealed by her jacket. As the arrogant sergeant's eyes grew big as dollars, without a moment of hesitation, the pistol discharged. The impact of the lead bullet knocked the man to the ground. The revolver continued to fire a second, third, and fourth bullet. With each explosion, fire and smoke spit from the instrument of death and another man was mortally dispatched to meet his destiny and the devil. The balance of the rabble ran like rabbits.

Diablo reared and struck a hoof into the face of the man who thought he had control of the animal's head. At Lupe's command, the stallion's hind hoofs dug into the dirt and he lunged forward. Once satisfied they had not been victims of the pistol, the gang regrouped, raised their muskets, and fired in Lupe's direction. She hunkered down in the saddle as the ill-aimed rifle shots whistled past her. When she was a safe distance away from the unfortunate band of un-merry men, she stopped. She poured water from her canteen into the palm of her hand. Diablo drank it, washing the froth from his tongue. She then kissed the horse's face.

"You are my brave, handsome boy." The horse's eyes rolled in his head. She then poured water onto a scrap of bandage she retrieved from her saddlebag and wiped the blood spatter from herself and Diablo. She had learned from her experience as a mother and nurse: wet blood cleans easily, dried blood does not.

CHAPTER 16

Lupe Returns to Caldera

"Lupe! Lupe!" was on the lips of everyone as she rode into the little village. Senora Hidalgo came out of her house as quickly as her cane would allow.

"Guadalupe, come inside. I have food ready, roasted chicken, fresh tortillas, salsa."

"Where is Juana, Mother?"

"She is hiding in Las Ollas. Federalies have been making surprise searches, looking for deserters and taking their supplies."

Lupe called aside one of the men from the assemblage of people who had come to welcome her home.

"Eduardo, here is an order from General Diaz. Stand by the corrals and show this to any army patrols. Tell them with force in your voice, they are not permitted to enter Caldera."

"Yes, Dona Lupe," she briefly thought about what she had heard him say. It was the first time the term had been directed to her.

"I'll be here with you tonight, Mother, I promise, but right now, I must go see Juana." She gave her mother a big hug before she rode Diablo to the entrance to Los Ollas.

"Juana?"

Juana peeked cautiously from behind a boulder at the entrance to the secret place.

"Lupe, we have been worried sick."

"Why would you worry about me?"

"There are soldiers wandering, looting, and raping. Thank God you're safe."

"Thanks to Dios and Diablo," Lupe said as she stroked her horse's face.

"Where are the Frenchmen?"

"They are all inside."

"How is the Colonel?"

"He hasn't awakened since the surgery. He stirs and talks in his dreams but that is all."

"What about the other men?"

"The wounded are healing well, all is good."

"Three weeks, it's a long time to sleep. Any day now, I think he'll be alright. Juana, I have the best news."

"Tell me."

"Vicente is well, and Escobedo. I found then in the dungeon at Chapultepec."

"Where is he?" Juana looked behind Lupe.

"He stayed in Mexico City to help organize the government."

"I'm so happy for you, Lupe. I have news too."

"What? Tell me, Hermana."

"Remember the French doctor?"

"Yes."

"I am in love with him."

Her eyes widened in surprise. "Juana, how did that happen? When did it happen?"

"How does it happen? It was like a magician's spell came over me. Here in Las Ollas."

The women hugged each other in excitement, transported back to when they were happy little girls playing games of husbands, love, romance, and marriage.

"Juana." Jean Pierre called as he approached them. "Hello, senora. When did you arrive?"

"Only this minute. Please monsieur, I am Lupe."

"De Vallier has opened his eyes," Jean advised Juana.

Lupe and Juana accompanied him to where the Colonel was reclined in the sulfuric waters of the hot springs. As they approached the old man, he looked up at Lupe. His eyes were tired yet tranquil and at peace.

"Guadalupe Hidalgo Martinez, tell me of my men." These were the last words he had said before descending into his coma and now they were the first words he said when he awoke.

"They are all well and safe, monsieur."

"Thank God for sending his angels to protect us," he said as he again closed his eyes in contentment.

CHAPTER 17

Oso Negro

"Make sure you are well hidden before the sun comes up. You must be ready for comancheros near the border," Lupe repeated the important topics as if she thought something was forgotten or that Juana wasn't paying attention.

"Go around the main towns."

"Lupe, how many times do you need to go over this? I have made the trip many times. I know the way. We will be alright. I know it is impossible for you not to worry, but your worrying is beginning to become a problem. I fully understand my mission and it is easy to accomplish."

"Sorry. I know you will be alright. It's just that there are so many to hide."

The moon was rising as the small caravan moved away from the safety of Caldera. Juana hugged Lupe before swinging up into the saddle. She waved and then rode out toward the front cart which was driven by Jean Pierre. Beside him sat Colonel de Vallier.

It was hot and would only get hotter as they moved North through the Sonora desert. The only shade was from sombreros and the canvas stretched over hoops which covered the carts. They brought carts instead of wagons to help make the group look rural and purely Mexican, without any hint of a foreign nature. The Legionnaires were all in peasant clothing and from a distance, no one would suspect. Juana wanted to be sure those who saw them kept their distance.

"Galveston seems a million miles away. How long will it take us to get there?" Jean Pierre asked Juana as she settled down with a plate of food the first night they camped.

"Twenty days if we travel on the road by day. If we push half-way through the night every other day, we can shave a few days off," Juana told him.

"If all the nights are like this one," the handsome Frenchman said, "I'll be happy every day." He surveyed the millions of stars which twinkled overhead, illuminating the landscape and lighting Juana's face softly. Juana's skin was not as soft or smooth as her younger sisters, but her facial features were strong and proud. Her eyes were clear and spoke of truth, honesty, hard work, and a childlike playful nature. Her body was not petite or overtly feminine like Lupe's, but her hips and breasts were proportional and even in pants and a muslin shirt, she could never be mistaken for anything other than a woman. Jean Pierre had recognized her beauty before now, but at this moment he found himself mesmerized by it.

"You are radiant this evening, Cheri," his words brought a smile to her lips. "Let's skip the campfire tonight." This suggestion was rewarded with a flirtatious glance.

The timing of the trip north was perfect, since the Mexican army was being reorganized by the General, now President Porfirio Diaz, and his commanders were in Mexico City receiving commissions and orders. The soldiers were at their villages, reacquainting with their families and the countryside was quiet. As the caravan approached the border to the United States, their main obstacle lay before them, Comancheros. They were a band of warriors with mixed Mexican and Apache blood who inhabited and controlled territory along the Mexican side of the border.

"We need to stop for an hour, so the horses can rest," Bernardo suggested. Juana knew he would not make the request if it were not necessary. Traveling at night took a toll on both the animals and humans.

"Make camp and double the guard. We're stopping for the night." Juana ordered.

They sat near the campfire talking about events of the day and planning the next.

"If they think we can be taken easily, they will attack us with some attempt of surprise. They want our horses, guns, carts, and they prize women and children for slaves. They know the land here and that gives them an advantage, but if we are ready when they attack, they will lose it. If they don't want to risk an attack, they will try bartering with us."

As the leaders of this company discussed matters of strategy and tactics, the answer to the question of how the commancheros were going to deal with them came into the camp. An arrow with an oil-soaked strip of cloth wrapped around the shaft and lit aflame, came whooshing past them and stuck into the side of one of the carts. The aim was so accurate that if the arrow was intended to be fatal, one of them would be mortally wounded.

"We have our answer," Bernardo said to Juana. "They want to talk."

Jean Pierre and Juana retreated to the comfort of the mattress lying on the floor of their cart. Juana had always prided herself and, being like her sister, she was able to sleep even when tensions were at their highest. It was clear to her that if she was needed, they would awaken her. For her to remain ever vigilant during a period of perilous circumstance was un-wise. After all, sleep-deprived people made mistakes rested people avoided.

Jean Pierre counted the hash marks he had made on a side of the cart.

"Seventeen days. How many more do you think it will be before we reach Galveston?"

"I fear the Comancheros might delay us and we could suffer losses."

"If we pay them, do you think they will allow us to continue without trouble?"

"We will see, now we must rest, Cheri," she said as she snuggled into his arms and allowed the warmth of his embrace to melt away the problems of the world.

* * * * *

Someone banged on the side of the cart several times and Juana leapt out the back. She had not undressed and hit the ground ready for action. Bernardino was riding toward camp at a full gallop from the ridgeline on the eastern horizon. He rode straight to where she stood and swung down urgently from the saddle.

"There's only sixteen of them and four are no more than boys, twelve warriors." Bernardino reported the news which heightened the spirits of all those gathered around.

"Are you sure? Are there two camps?"

"No. I'm certain of it."

"Our numbers are six to their one; do you think they know that?" Juana asked.

"They have had opportunity to observe us, but they do not know we are soldiers. Yet they are cautious because they are shorthanded.

"Juana, you better come!" a voice called.

Juana stepped toward the call and saw the silhouettes of six mounted men, their horses standing in the road about one hundred and fifty yards ahead. Although slightly beyond visibility, it was easy to know they were heavily armed. Jean Pierre and Juana stood gazing at the spectacle of bright red, blue, and green cloth, which punctuated their tribal costumes, their uncut black hair flowing out of colorful headscarves.

After they had formulated a quick plan, Juana called for horses. She, Bernardo, and Jean Pierre rode out under a white flag to meet with the delegation that stood in their road.

When they were within hearing, the comancheros leader spoke out. "Buenos Dias, it's a glorious day, a good day to die, wouldn't you say? Perhaps you have heard of me, I am 'Oso Negro' and these men are the toll collectors. We collect a small toll from everyone who passes by on this road. The toll is one half of your money, horses, guns, and ammunition. If you do not wish to pay, it's OKAY but you will have to turn back. I think you must have heard of me, or why else would you men have brought me such a beautiful present?" The scarred face leader of this band chuckled, eyeing Juana greedily.

Jean Pierre and Bernardino exchanged a quick glance and then both smiled toothy grins, turning to look at the leader of this posse of misfits.

Bernardino spoke out, "It is my pleasure to introduce to you our commandante, Senorita Juana Hidalgo and might I suggest it is in your best interest to listen very carefully to what she has to say, senor toll collector."

The once pompous smile on the scarred face sagged into a vicious snarl.

"Senor, we are aware that your warriors are but sixteen souls and four of those are barely considered men. I feel it my duty to inform you that among us are eighty-one well trained, well-armed, professional soldiers. We have prepared a small demonstration to help you decide how you will conduct your business on this glorious day, which is, as you say, a good day to die."

Jean Pierre lowered the lance pole and removed the white flag. He replaced it with a wooden target shaped like a man's head. Ears, eyes, a nose, and a smile were drawn on the wood with a piece of charcoal. Jean hoisted the target into the air and six men in Legionnaire uniforms with white leather caps marched from the ranks of the people who stood near the carts one hundred fifty yard away. The soldiers halted and knelt, raising their muskets. Six puffs of white smoke were visible. Six bullets struck the target before the crackling report of the rifles pounded the air. Jean Pierre lowered the target and displayed it to the awestruck desperados. The target had six bullet holes in it. One hole was between the eyes, one in the left eye, one in the nose, two in the mouth and one had blown off the right ear.

Juana spoke, "We have already decided to spare your lives unless you speak one word of a threat or make a demand, or if you attempt to block our passage. We will shoot any one of you who comes within our range. Do I make myself clear, Senor Oso Negro?"

Reluctantly, the answer came. "Yes, Senorita."

"Very well, you may go. May the grace and peace of Virgin go with you and be with your people."

"Equalemente, senorita," Oso Negro said as he and his riders turned, galloping away, soon vanishing into a cloud of dust.

CHAPTER 18

The Proposal

The days spent in Galveston were busy. Sending telegrams, obtaining travel documents, attending to matters related to quartering soldiers in a foreign city. After receiving letters of credit, guaranteed by the government of France, Galveston was also a time of restaurant dining rooms, evening strolls along wooden sidewalks, passing shop windows that displayed unimaginable things to a girl from a small rural pueblo in the remoteness of Mexico. It was a time of hotel parlors and a room with a feather bed where Juana and Jean Pierre engaged each other as man and woman.

Jean Pierre sat savoring his coffee in the dining room of the Hotel Valdez, gazing out the window at the business of the seaport. Colonel De Vallier entered and sat down.

"Passage is arranged. We sail upon the tide at two in the morning on the Fleurs-de-Lis out of New Orleans. She's carrying a cargo of cotton to

Marseilles. She has no cabins, but the captain will make room for us in the hold. Notify the men to muster on the pier at midnight."

The words struck Jean Pierre like a hammer between his eyes.

"Colonel, after issuing the orders for the men, may I take leave until midnight?" he asked.

The Colonel looked toward his lieutenant. There was no need for explanation. He knew there was a chance it would be the last time he ever saw the young man again. How many chapters are written in the age-old story about a soldier who abandoned his post and company, to live his life in a foreign land, in love with a native girl?

"Be on board by midnight. Keep your wits about you man, you have responsibilities."

"Yes sir, I will sir," came the quick reply.

* * * * *

The moment he opened the door, she sensed it. A horror-stricken pallor drained her face of color as she looked at him. She clung to him and began to cry. He kissed her mouth, wet with salty, sugar-sweet tears.

"Don't cry, Cheri."

"We will never see each other again," her voice choked with emotion.

"Juana Hidalgo, will you marry me?" he asked as he knelt on one knee clutching her skirt, looking up into her eyes, eyes which were cavernous, eyes sparkling with excitement and anticipation at the suggestion of an entire life with him.

"Yes, I will marry you," she said reaching down, taking his face in her hands, pulling him up and kissing him hard on the mouth.

"You'll go with me, to Paris. You'll love it."

"Yes, I will love anywhere you take me, but I'll love you and our child more," she said as she brushed her hand down across her stomach.

Jean's eyes told of the excitement a man has when he learns the woman he loves is carrying his child. He returned to his knees and laid his cheek against her stomach.

"Why didn't you tell me?" he asked, looking up.

"You were leaving, and I didn't want you to ever think I stole your life by tricking you into staying with me."

"My God, what thoughts are inside that pretty head of yours? I love you, Juanita."

"A woman is always insecure."

"Forgive me now and forevermore, if I forget to tell you enough times or my actions fall short of proving it, for it is my desire that you know, as long as there is breath in my body, I will love you, and after that, so long as there is a heaven and hell, I will love you. Tell me you forgive me for making you so unsure."

"I forgive you, you silly man," she said, laughing happily as she fell backward onto the bed, positioning her skirt in a way she knew would seduce him.

CHAPTER 19

Children of the Witch

A t precisely two in the morning, the Fleurs-de-lis raised the gangplank from the dock and the sailors began preparing to shove off. Jean Pierre was not yet aboard. Colonel De Vallier resolved that he could live with this disappointment and went below to his berth in the Captain's cabin.

When the sun rose the next morning, the ship's sails were full of wind blowing toward the horizon. Galveston was long since twinkling lights off the stern that completely faded into the black line of the horizon. The Colonel was ecstatic at the news that Jean Pierre had indeed come aboard. The reason for his delay was that he and Juana had difficulty finding Nanita, Juana's friend and companion, but she was found and the three barely made it on board before the ship sailed away from the dock.

The Colonel was delighted to see the woman to whom they all owed so much, more than they could ever repay.

October 29, 1869, the logbook of Capitan Claude Reniot, Sailing Master of the good ship Fleurs-de-Lis did report: "Witnessed by an assemblage of the seamen and passengers, with a choir of gulls crying celebration overhead, with Colonel Jacques de Vallier standing as groomsman and Nanita Gonzales as brides maid, I presided at and certified the marriage of Jean Pierre Farre' and Juanita Hidalgo Farre'."

That night the passengers and crew all slept on pallets or in hammocks on deck, so the Farre's had privacy, a broken-open bale of cargo making a wonderfully soft love-nest.

* * * * *

On the fourth evening of the voyage, the newlyweds stood on the quarter-deck.

"I can see what draws a man to sea," Juana said as she gazed at the star-filled sky that seemed so close, they could be touched.

"The sea is so calm and beautiful, the air so soft and sweet it makes me feel wonderful." Juana said to Jean.

One of the sailors attending to his duty overheard her and stepped near. He looked at the same array of stars and calm sea, but in his eyes was only fear.

"When it gets like this, there's trouble ahead, Miss. You'd best find a good place below where you can batten yourself down, to ride her out."

"In heaven's name man, mind your tongue. Don't scare the lady, the weather couldn't be more perfect," Jean Pierre snapped.

"Tis the quiet that lies before a storm, lad. Best heed me words, rough seas lie ahead. Find a good place below, because we're in for it, sure as my name be Finbar and that there be the North Star," the old man pointed a gnarled finger toward Polaris.

"She's a big seaworthy ship, we have nothing to fear," Jean Pierre said profoundly.

The sailor looked square at Jean. Salt and pepper spiced the old man's beard. Tobacco, coffee, and rum stained his teeth, and his eyes bespoke nothing but experience and truth.

"She's big now but wait till the wind's blowing so hard it can snatch a man off her deck like he is nothing but a feather and the waves are higher than her masts, then you'll think you be riding a cork that just popped out of a bottle. Mark my words, we're sailing into it. I've seen this before."

As if the old man's words were spellbinding, the glow in the night sky began to darken and the sails began to stiffen against the increasing wind. Within hours Juana and Jean could see that what was foretold was coming upon them. The beautiful star-filled sky was swallowed up by ominous darkness. Huge waves began to pound against the hull of the ship, pushing her in directions she didn't want to go, unnatural ways which caused her to pop and creak, cry, and moan, reviling the sea which was regurgitating spray and big droplets of salt water into the air. When the water was caught in the gale force of the winds, it hit hard as pebbles and the spray grated like sandpaper on the skin and in the eyes of those who were desperately trying to keep the ship on course. Course had to be maintained to keep the sea from completely having its way with the ship and laying claim to her, the valuable cargo and the precious souls aboard.

"Get below and stay below! Don't get near the cargo! It'll fly all over. You'll be crushed if you're not careful," Finbar yelled against the gale.

One hundred and thirty-five feet from stem to stern, the Fleurs-de-Lis balanced on the crest of each wave, then she tipped forward, rocketed down deep into the trough, separating the giant waves. At the bottom, she crashed into the front side of another swell and there her timbers would scream and moan as her bow raised up and began the laborious climb, slicing up the wall of water, fighting to get back to the top. Thousands of gallons of water washed over the decks, sweeping the tethered sailors off their feet. Tons of water was fighting against their grip, trying to harvest the men into the deep.

Jean Pierre and Juana had wrapped themselves in several quilts and snuggled into a berth designed for rations. A thunderous, crashing boom was accompanied by a percussion which ran through every board and timber of the ship. The hatch cover slid open and Finbar stood at the head of the focsle.

"All hands on deck! Bring ye axes. The mizzen mast's down. Hack her away lads, clear the deck. Save the ship!" Finbar shouted.

Jean Pierre and Juana joined the line of men scrambling up the ladder. The moment they set foot on the planks of the deck, a wave crested the starboard side knocking them both down and washed them, clutching each other, against the port side gunwale. Out of the watery mist, Finbar appeared and handed a line to Jean.

"Tie this around your waist." The old sailor commanded. He then tied a line around Juana's waist. He attached the tethers to the jackline that was lashed from fore to aft down the center of the ship. Ten feet away, the helmsman called out.

"Mr. Cross, I need help here, I can't hold her." As he finished his sentence, a twenty-foot length of two-inch rope came whipping through the air, catching him across the neck. He and the rope disappeared into the mist. The helm began to spin, and the ship listed hard. Finbar grabbed hold of the big wheel and strained to stop it. He called to Jean.

"Lend a hand!"

Jean and Juana struggled, pulling on the tethers to climb away from the rail listing deep into the raging water. They both took hold of the handles at the end of spokes of the big wheel. The three of them put every ounce of strength they had against the strain and forced the wheel around till the ship righted and the deck leveled. Had that feat of super-human determination not been accomplished at that moment, the ship would have foundered.

Finbar pointed to the compass housed inside the binnacle upon which the large wheel was mounted. Amazingly, the small carbide flame was still burning, flickering light onto the compass which was rocking wildly as the ship bucked and rolled.

"Hold two twenty-five, mate." Finbar finished the words, turned, began yelling orders and was gone.

Juana and Jean fought the huge wheel. Holding as close to two hundred and twenty-five degrees as possible, while the crew fought to keep the ship functioning, they fought the battle for survival against their lover, the sea. The raging sea that articulates the human condition, it is the lover who is the most passionate giver of pleasure who is the most unsympathetic taker of life.

Hour after hour the ship and her sons of the sea fought the raging water and as if Poseidon waved his scepter, conceding this ship and crew were worthy, the torment subsided, and the course became manageable once more. Although damaged, the Fleurs-de-Lis began to sail hard and fast, toward the orange glow on the horizon as the morning sunrise neared.

Tired to the marrow of his bones, even so, Jean Pierre felt strong, well and alive. He held the helm with his left hand, Juana held it with her right, and they held each other with arms outstretched.

Finbar approached, "You two had a hand in it, make no mistake, your lives 'll never be the same. You've seen the witch and she's made you her children."

Finbar appointed a man to relieve them at the helm. "Now go below and get some sleep. That's an order."

CHAPTER 20

Rancho Martinez de Caldera

L ife had returned with the war-weary army to the Hacienda Escobedo. The wounded had been nursed back to health. The happiness that had always been a hallmark of this rancho was back. Gaiety and festivity were once again subjects for planning, along with building projects, planting the crops, and breeding the herds.

"I want that wall pushed out twenty feet. The veranda expanded double. There will be a hundred for dinner and another hundred will arrive for the dancing. They should not feel cramped. Many of the guests are coming from the capitol and the United States. I want Cinco de Mayo to be a memory they will never forget." Don Escobedo declared to Lupe.

When the evening finally arrived, Lupe was the person in charge of the staff in the household, all of whom were exceedingly busy serving the needs of so many guests. This did not preclude her and Vicente from being among the guests enjoying the party. Don

Escobedo had made it clear that it was his wish for it to be so.

The music stopped, and the beautifully colored twirling skirts of the dancers came to rest, the crowd began to chatter.

"Ladies and Gentlemen, your attention please," the orchestra leader quieted the audience. "Don Escobedo has an announcement to make."

Don Escobedo climbed onto the raised orchestra platform.

"Actually, what I have is a presentation. This is a great day for the people of Mexico. I don't think we will ever forget to celebrate our victory over the French on the fifth of May. Most of you had a hand in the victory we are gathered to celebrate. To each other, we owe many debts. I request that we all bow our heads for a moment to remember those we knew, who are not here because they paid the supreme price so that we might be here tonight as free Mexicans.

All in attendance became solemn and handkerchiefs were handed from gentlemen to ladies as tears were wiped away.

"I thank each one of you in this room who had a hand in our victory. To those who have received medals and commendations from the government in the capital, I add my congratulations to the well-deserved testaments of your sacrifice, courage, and determination. At this time, I would like to make a special presentation. Would Vicente and Guadalupe Martinez please come here and join me?"

The couple stepped out of the crowd and Don Escobedo took Lupe's hand and helped her up onto the platform. As the patron beamed with pride, he handed Vicente a rolled parchment tied with silk ribbon.

"On behalf of my family and the people of Mexico, I present to you, Vicente and Guadalupe Martinez, one thousand acres of land surrounding the Pueblo Caldera and surrender to you all rights, claims and privileges that go with this Rancho Martinez de Caldera."

As Lupe folded forward into Vicente's arms, the room around them exploded with cheers and applause. Every person in the room felt like part of the giving of this unbelievable gift and they all were ecstatically happy for this young couple.

CHAPTER 21

Paris, France

Upon their arrival in France, the Farre' family insisted upon a grand wedding and there was no extravagance conceivable which was not provided. This event set a stage for Juana, and thereafter her days and nights took on an added enchantment by the fact she lived with a man she loved and who loved her in return. Although she often thought of her family and friends, there was no regret associated with her decision to leave that life and start a new one in a new country, with the new name bestowed upon her, Jacqueline Farre'.

The salons and societies of Paris became the social stage upon which the life of Jacqueline Farre' unfolded, and although she possessed neither fair hair nor snowy complexion so highly valued by the French, the currency of the Farre' name purchased much. She quickly acquired the customs and language of court. Her elegance and eloquence were equally rewarded with an ever-increasing circle of friends and acquaintances.

"Jacqueline," Madame Elysees called out as Juana was leaving the tearoom Cilice, one of the city's most elegant afternoon distractions. "I am having a recital at my salon on the 20th. I do hope you and Jean can attend. I'm introducing a new composer. It will be a gala I'm sure you will enjoy."

"I will ask my husband. It sounds like something we would enjoy, madame."

"Oh, that would be wonderful. Hope to see you then." The old crone returned to her covey of friends.

Madame Elysees was one of the premiere salons in Paris and patron to the hottest new artists and composers presenting work of the renaissance.

On the 20th, Jacqueline and Nanita arrived early and stood in the opulent parlor conversing with Madame Elysees.

"Oh no!" the elderly woman exclaimed.

"What is it?"

"Juliet Russo," the hostess whispered, motioning to a trio of women huddled together, occasionally casting leers in their direction. "She was expected to become engaged to Jean Pierre before he left for Mexico. Uh, oh, here she comes."

As Juliet crossed the room, the wooden heels of satin shoes decorated with rhinestones clacked loudly, purposefully announcing her every move. Her neck swayed to and fro, balancing a coiffure of white curls standing eight inches above her head, deeply rouged pursed lips, talc powder caked on her forehead so thick and smooth a quill could be employed to draft a message on it.

"So, I finally meet the one whose name exudes abundantly past so many lips," she quipped.

"It is good to meet you, Mademoiselle. I am Jacqueline Farre." Juana extended a hand, which was ignored.

"The name, to which I refer, a rather vulgar one, Juana, I believe. Are you not she, senora?" Juliet's words spit from her mouth like bullets, spit from the barrel of a dueling brace.

"From my husband and family, I often hear that name. As for you and your company, you may address me as 'Jacqueline'."

"Yes, yes, it is my understanding that you acquired this name, Jacqueline; Jacqueline Farre, and a family fortune by means of imposition."

"Speak plainly to me, Mademoiselle, or hold your tongue." The words eloquently spoken by Jacqueline with the forcefulness that was purely Juanita Hidalgo.

"Is it not true that you imposed upon a gentleman the duty required of a father, and thereby acquired a husband, his fortune, and family?"

A fist was made but the desire to strike was held in check. The fire in Juana's eyes could have burned holes through the pasty, powdered, perfumed young woman. Several seconds of tension were broken.

"There was nothing imposed, Mademoiselle, only marriage proposed, by a man who was in love, and had not the knowledge of the blessing which would be bestowed upon him by the birth of his son. Now, if you will excuse me, I see that my husband has arrived." She curtsied and stepped past Juliet.

As Juliet turned, attempting to display some attention toward Jean Pierre, Nanita took her arm and pulled her close. "I was present when my mistress used a chivota, a small knife we use in my country for butchering goats, sharp as a razor, to sever the vocal cords of an enemy sentry who was about to shout an alarm, exposing my mistress and those in her charge to danger. I would choose my words more carefully if I were you." Then, with a very condescending tone, "Mademoiselle." Nanita pushed Juliet away with such force that she staggered harshly, trying to stay upright in her rhinestone-encrusted, satin shoes. Her coiffure, being not so fortunate, tumbled over. Juliet, grappling her hair, went scurrying toward the powder room with her entourage clambering behind her.

"I do not know what you ever saw in that woman," Juana said to Jean Pierre.

"What woman, Cheri?"

"Juliet."

"I really couldn't say, because I don't remember a Juliet, did you say?"

"You are so diplomatic, and handsome," Juana kissed Jean on his cheek.

"I have wonderful news, at least I think you will approve."

"What? Please tell me."

"De Vallier is going to Mexico, and I agreed that we would accompany him."

"Please, tell me it's true. When?"

"We leave in two weeks to the coast and then we will sail. But really it is not sailing. We will go on the new steam ship. It only takes six days to cross."

"We don't even have time to send word to my sister that we are coming."

"De Vallier has sent a dispatch by diplomatic courier. They will be expecting us, Cheri."

Juana turned and rushed across the room, "Nanita, we're going home!"

CHAPTER 22

Welcome Home

L upe stood on the porch watching the sun cresting the wildflower-covered hills, bringing with its rays an anticipation that triggered memories from her youth; memories of the day she stood as a young woman and eagerly awaited a sign of the caravan carrying Vicente to her. Today, the coach coming over those hills would carry Juana. Lupe had not seen her sister for five years. Lupe's heart fluttered at the thought of seeing her sister's child. She thought about how surprised Juana would be to see the transformation of their little village into the Rancho Hidalgo Martinez de Caldera.

Vicente came out of the house and stood alongside her. He placed his arm across her shoulder.

"Be still, mi rosa. They will not arrive for a few hours."

"I know, but I just can't help being excited," she said.

"Have I ever told you that your happiness is what makes me happy?"

"No. I don't think I've heard you say that before," Lupe said as she looked to her husband with joy.

"Good."

"Good? How is it good?"

"Because, from now on I am going to find a new way, every day, to tell you I love you."

"Do you know you make my heart bigger when you say such things?" she asked, taking his hand and placing it on her breast.

"Yes, I can feel that," Vicente grinned as he gently caressed her breast.

Lupe took his wrist, and raised his hand and kissed his palm, "Not now, mi amour, not now."

"Will your sister recognize the place?"

"She will, and she will enjoy learning about every detail of how we have built it, for that I am I'm sure."

"Will you ask her to stay here and live with us?"

"Yes, but you must speak with her husband about the things men speak of regarding such a thing."

"I cannot describe the aromas drifting in the air in spring or the happiness at seeing a calf emerge from its mother's womb, nor can I explain how the music at the Festival de la Vacca's makes a man feel. He must see for himself the colors God uses to paint in the sky as the sun rises and sets. How can I tell him about the temperature in the pools of the caverns or how the water can take away any pain or sorrow that a person might feel? There are times when words are of no value."

"Los Ollas, he knows," Lupe said. "Juana told me it is where they fell in love. It is where they made love for the first time."

"Then this man and I are like brothers who share fondly a common memory."

"Have you ever thought of writing down some of those memories? In these moments, you are such a romantic. If you could capture these emotions, express your feelings on paper, your words would lighten the hearts of many who have not experienced the awe, the wonder, the true happiness of falling into and being in love," she said kissing his lips.

"Know this one thing, Corazon, the longer your sister and her husband stay with us, the more they will learn to love the life here. Each new day brings with it the chance of them staying. The longer they live here, the desire to remain multiplies."

"The things you say are true, as they usually are."

"Usually, you mean 'always'."

"Well, almost, always," Lupe said laughing as a loud chime signaled that the morning meal was ready to be served.

"Let's go and eat now, or shall we go and take a little morning nap?" Vicente asked as he pulled Lupe tight into his arms.

"Maybe a little nap in the afternoon, mi amour," Lupe said as she pulled away from his embrace and entered the house.

* * * * *

"Please pass the ham," Diego said.

"Why are you devouring your food like a hungry dog? Slow down, chew each bite, enjoy your food. Eating this way is not healthy for you," Vicente scolded.

"I am hurrying, so I can ride out and meet Aunt Juana. I want to see my cousin, Jean Pierre."

"Take one thing at a time, my Son. You do not need to hurry. You know the routine of the journey here from Escobedo's. They are still two hours away, only now watering their horses at the pool in the three rocks."

"Yes, I know, Father. But the sooner I leave, the sooner I will see them. Is that not true?"

He chuckled. "Your logic cannot be argued with, however the truth of it does not lessen the importance of you not gobbling down your food, my son. Many things are mutually true."

"Did you always understand things so easily, Father?"

"When I was your age, your grandfather spoke to me of truth and he helped me to see that there can be many truths at one time. A person must not only see what is obvious but search out what is obscure.

This is necessary for us to have good judgment. It is the cornerstone of our personal safety, that of our people, and the safety of our animals. Grandfather told me, 'Listen quietly and you will hear whispers of the truth in your mind'. Regardless of how circumstance rage around you, the voice of the truth can always be heard, if you will only listen."

"I will, Father."

"You are a good son. I am very proud of you."

"Thank you, Father."

"Now go, you may take Diablo, ride like the wind and bring our family home."

CHAPTER 23

The Guests

The customary shot was fired when the stagecoach was in range of being heard. Every soul awakened and began stirring at the prospect of Juana's return. When the bell in the church began clanging, people came streaming out of their houses, from every direction, as the coach come rolling across the yard to the front of the big house.

"Whoa," the driver called to the team of four well matched horses, pulling on the reins as the stage came to a halt. A steady parade ran through the village waving and calling out greetings to the visitors.

The driver began throwing off bags, cartons, and luggage into the waiting arms of men eager to carry them into the house. Vicente opened the door of the iron wheeled coach and took Juana's hand as she climbed down gracefully, followed immediately by Jean Pierre, who in turn helped their four-year-old son down. Next from the coach emerged the Colonel, who had put on his tunic and was in full dress uniform. The fine Parisian styling worn by Juana immediately became the topic of conversation as the entourage made way through the arched entryway and into the house.

As the luggage was triaged, the Colonel gave special attention to the chest containing gifts brought from France. "I want to keep this one close at hand."

"Romero, Mario, carry this one to the Sala Verde," Vicente instructed the young men holding the handles of the large wooden trunk bound with plates of metal and securely closed with straps of leather buckled on top.

Vicente led the Colonel into the parlor, barely able to contain himself, wanting to acquire information regarding the developments in politics and science taking place in the outside world.

"The Americans seem to be everywhere in the capital. Do they come here?" the Colonel asked.

"No, but the American brand of English language is commonly spoken in the Casa de Escobedo.

"Yes. I experienced that as we stayed overnight on our journey here. There were several Americans in residence."

"How is Senor Escobedo?"

"He's fine. Complains a bit about the pain in the leg where he was wounded. He claims he knows I am the one who shot him. He laughs madly when he tells the story."

"The Yankees have no business with us, and we want to keep it that way. It's quiet here, as you soon will learn, and I hope, begin to appreciate." Vicente reported.

"I expect that will all change shortly."

"What do you mean?"

"I don't want to steal Jean Pierre's thunder. Here, I brought these for you." The Colonel went into the trunk and withdrew a handful of cigars tied together with a ribbon of linen. "I got these in Vera Cruz. They're from Cuba. I thought they were exceptionally good, and this to go along with them." Reaching again into the box, he withdrew a bottle of French cognac.

Diego, young Jean Pierre, and Carmen came bursting into the room.

"Diego, I have brought some things for you to enjoy," the Colonel said as he went back into the trunk and withdrew a stack of books. "I hope you read the French language?"

"Yes, Monsieur, I read French, English, and as a consolation, of course, Spanish."

"What a bright young man, most excellent indeed. You and I must speak of your coming to France, where you can attend to your education at Academy Saint Cyr L'ecole. It is the finest academy in all of France. The best officers from every army around the globe are being trained there. I hold a faculty post and your admittance is a certainty. Of course, you would live in my home with me while you study."

Diego looked toward his father. Vicente could see the excitement on his son's face at the thought of such an adventure.

"We will have time to speak of this." Vicente said softly.

As Vicente spoke, the Colonel went back into the large box and withdrew a small box carefully wrapped in royal blue silk, tied with red silk ribbon. "This, dear, is for you," and handed the box to Carmen. She curtsied as she accepted the present and sat on the sofa before opening it. Lifting of the lid revealed a string of pearls. The radiance and luster of the white orbs was reflected on her face as her complexion took on a similar aura.

"Thank you, Monsieur. I will wear these for my Quinceanera. Mother, look what a marvelous gift Monsieur de Vallier has brought for me," Carmen said as Juana and Lupe entered the room.

The Colonel, now completely caught up in the spirit of giving gifts, once again went into the chest to withdraw an evening gown. When he held it up for display, Lupe instinctively knew it was for her. She and Juana began speaking praises to dress, about its Parisian styling, how sheer the fabric was, what care had gone into its hand stitched appointments and the radiance of the color.

"Thank you, Monsieur," Lupe said sincerely. "And I have something for you. Excuse me for a moment, I will get it," Lupe said as she left the room, taking her gown with her. She returned a few minutes later, carrying the silver case containing the sword with a gold handle that was presented to her the day she accepted the surrender. She held it out toward the Colonel in formal presentation.

"No, No, I can't accept that. It is yours. You must keep it," the Colonel lowered his head as if he were feeling echoes of the pain from that fateful day.

"Monsieur, this symbol of your honor was presented to you by your country, but it does not really belong to you. It belongs to your family. It has been my privilege to keep it safe for you here, and now it is my duty to return it. There is no honor in my keeping it. It would be my honor if you would accept it."

A shudder of emotion was visible as tears appeared in the old man's eyes. He took the gold handled sword, which had his name engraved along the side of its case and slid it through the ring on his belt, which had been empty these past five years. He felt as if the emptiness in his soul had finally been filled. Stepping toward Lupe, he embraced her as a father embraces a daughter.

"Thank you, dear child," the old man said as he hugged her tightly.

CHAPTER 24

The Big News

The aroma created by activities in the kitchen preceded the arrival of the food as news of a victory precedes the return of an army, and the people who came with the food were greeted like heroes returning victorious from a foreign campaign.

The twenty who assembled to dine wore their finest. The blend of the latest from Paris and traditional Mexican formalwear, having crepes next to the tortillas and hearing English, French, and Spanish spoken by those conversing, combined to mark the occasion with an air of sophistication and gaiety.

After the meal was presented, the food and all who were about to partake of it were blessed. Vicente leaned toward Jean and said, "I am told you have some news, very exciting news, to be exact, that you wish to share with us, Monsieur Jean Pierre."

"I am waiting for the right moment. Perhaps it is now," the Frenchman said. He withdrew a red silk cloth from his pocket and unwrapped it. Inside it was a rock. He proudly handed the cloth, with the stone presented on it, to Vicente.

Vicente passed a critical eye over the rock, then his facial expression displayed curiosity and with a slight tilting of his head, he gave a sideways glance toward his guest.

"I'm not quite sure I understand, Monsieur. You may have to explain."

"Senor, prior to being inducted into the service, I was a student at the Institute Polytechnic at Paris, preparing for a career as a doctor. There, I did some studies in geology. While in the custody of your people, hiding in the caverns near here, I recognized what seemed to be classic examples of mineral strata consistent with formations of silver oxide. I brought a field assay kit with me on this visit and Juana and I went to Los Ollas yesterday. I had the opportunity to explore the cave system and run a few tests. Based upon my calculations, it is possible, that your 'Ollas' may contain the largest deposit of silver ever to be discovered in Mexico, or anywhere else for that matter."

Vicente sat back in his seat, inspecting the ore sample, startled by this news. He folded the cloth securely around the precious lump and placed it into the breast pocket of his jacket

"Monsieur, who, besides yourself has knowledge of this?"

"Juana and General de Vallier."

"The Colonel?"

"Actually, the courier who arrived today brought a dispatch advising that his rank has been elevated. He is now a General. There was also some business related to your wife."

"What would that be?"

"I am not privileged to know."

"Monsieur, I would greatly appreciate your confidence in the matter regarding the Ollas. Speak to no one. May I have your pledge."

"Indeed, sir, my word is given."

"Thank you, Monsieur, for this wonderful news."

Vicente rose and began striking the side of his water glass with a knife. The ringing brought the buzz of conversation to a halt and all attention turned to him. Placing his water glass on the table and raising his wine glass, he spoke in a loud voice, "Damas y Caballeros, Ladies and gentlemen, Mademoiselles and Monsieurs, I have a most important announcement. I have just learned from my brother-in-law and guest," Vicente gestured to Jean Pierre, acknowledging him as the source of the information, "a piece of news that will be of interest to you all. We must stop referring to Monsieur de Vallier as Colonel de Vallier, as his rank has appreciated to that of a General. Would you all please stand and join me as I present this toast to General de Vallier."

The party rose with cheers and shouts of congratulations as they raised their glasses for the first of many toasts to come.

CHAPTER 25

No Good Can Come of This

Vicente and Lupe's home was constructed so that a gentle light filtered into their bedroom, announcing the coming of the morning. In the warm radiance of this morning light, Vicente did as he so often did, and lifted the sheet to gaze upon Lupe's body as she lay sleeping. His heart was filled with the same raging desire he always felt while looking at the pure beauty of her. Each time he performed this ritual, his heart was filled with gratitude that this woman, this goddess, was his, lying in his bed, naked and available. This feeling was the passion that drove his world.

Vicente lay back on his pillow, allowing his body and mind to enjoy the feeling a man has, when he has everything he ever wanted. Because of this truth the world is his oyster. As these feelings washed through his body, he saw a hand, followed by an arm clothed in a man's shirt sleeve, come out from the curtain that hung across the closet and reach into the breast pocket of the jacket draped across the back of a chair. The fingers attached to the hand nimbly withdrew the red silk cloth containing the silver ore. The hand then receded back into the closet. Vicente silently reached up and withdrew a pistol from the gun belt that hung on the bedpost. The silence in the room was broken by the unmistakable, almost thunderous sound of the hammer of the Colt revolver being drawn back, cocking and locking as the cylinder turned, advancing the cartridge into position under the firing pin.

"Step out from behind the curtain. I will not ask you again and if you do not, I will shoot you where you stand." There was no waver in Vicente's voice. As each second passed, time ticked with anticipation that he would have to fulfill his promise and pull the trigger.

"Momma." The door opened and Vicente's attention was drawn away from the closet and to Carmen as she stepped into the bedroom.

As quickly as a magician moves the moment his trick culminates, the body once hidden in the closet, became the man who was holding his daughter. One arm across her chest, its hand clutching the red silk cloth containing the precious metal. The other hand held the blade of a chivota at the throat of precious Carmen.

Carmen screamed.

Lupe awoke, and she also screamed. The two screams stopped at the exact moment, as if a maestro had swung down his baton.

Vicente jumped out of bed, never lowering the pistol which was pointed at the man who he now recognized as Juventino, one of the vaqueros.

"Tino, release her. I will not harm you if you do it now."

"Put down your gun, Senor, or I will bleed her like a goat," Tino said as he shook Carmen's body.

"You do not get chances in this game you play," Vicente said as he took one pace forward and fired a bullet, tearing into Tino's shoulder, causing the arm with the knife to fall limp. As the blade fell away, the father took another step toward his daughter and fired another shot, striking Juventino in the center of his forehead. The blow of this bullet knocked Tino away from Carmen and against the wall.

With one long stride, Vicente scooped his daughter into his arms as she fainted. Tino's body slumped down the wall into a pile on the floor, smearing blood on the wall as it went down.

Vicente carried Carmen to Lupe and then went to Tino's gasping, twitching body suspended briefly between life and death. The sky-blue eyes were still wide open and looked at Vicente as he approached and took possession of the red cloth containing the piece of rock. A stone thought to be so valuable that a young man, a man who was full of promise and honor, would lose his life trying to own it.

Vicente looked at the little package with disgust and concealed it in his palm as Juana and Jean Pierre rushed into the room from their quarters across the hall. Vicente ordered the hallway sealed to stop the clamor caused by all who heard the pistol's discharge and came running.

Vicente squeezed the rock hard as he looked at the dead boy, thinking silently as his head shook in disappointment, 'no good can ever come of this.'

CHAPTER 26

The New Discovery

Silver conches adorned the leather of the Charro outfit that displayed the supple outline of Lupe's figure. The wooden heels of her riding boots clacked on the terrazzo as she paced the office floor.

"Be still, mi rosa. Sit, calm yourself."

"Good morning," General de Vallier offered as he entered the room, followed by Jean Pierre.

"Please, shut the door. Please sit."

The four sat in stuffed leather chairs surrounding a large plank coffee table on which they placed their boots as was the custom when reclining into the comfort of these chairs. Jean Pierre began their meeting.

"The young man, Tino, accompanied us, Juana and me. He carried the equipment when we explored the 'Ollas'. I suppose he knew from our excitement after conducting the field tests on the ore samples that we had discovered something of value. Dreadful."

"Are you quite sure no one else was made aware of your discovery?"

"Juana and I have discussed this, and we are sure as we can be that no one else should have knowledge."

"This is good. We can only hope that Tino did not speak of this to anyone."

Three brief knocks sounded on the door.

"Enter," Vicente called to the door.

Dona Martinez came in, walking with the aid of her canes.

"Please sit Mother," Lupe stood and offered her seat.

"Thank you, Niña, I will stand. I shall only be a minute. I know you have many important things to discuss." She turned her attention to the Frenchmen.

"Our people have known from the time they first came to Caldera what you are now calling a great discovery. My husband, God give rest to his soul in heaven, took silver from Los Ollas to the market many years ago and purchased two healthy cows. He could have bought a thousand cows, but he made a humble, unassuming purchase; two cows, a few chickens, and a goat. With these, people can live with dignity and kindness, and community."

The old woman bowed her head for a moment as she gathered her thoughts and then raised her wrinkled, pleasant face and continued.

"Men and women who dig in a mine, live a dark, cold, pitiful life, producing a thing that does not live, and neither do they live fully. When the value of a person who digs rocks is reduced below the value of what he digs, he is worse off than a beast of burden. The burro feels the warmth of the sun on its skin, the earth beneath its hooves. He breathes fresh air when he carries the burden. I remember when my mother said to us, 'We cannot make tortillas with these rocks.' She was wise. That is all I have to say." The old woman turned and hobbled to the door.

"Thank you, Mother," Lupe said as her mother left the room, closing the door behind her.

Lupe and Vicente looked at each other. Vicente said, "Go ahead, mi amore."

"What we want to tell you is that we do not wish to harvest any ore from Los Ollas, nor do we wish knowledge of the existence to get out. My mother has so eloquently expressed our reasoning. We hope you understand. We have everything here that we could ever want. If word got out about the silver, I fear no gain could ever be worth what would be lost forever."

Vicente reached out and took Lupe's hand, giving it a gentle squeeze.

The General spoke up immediately, "This decision is yours and yours alone to make. I give my oath that no word of this will ever be spoken by me."

Jean Pierre's voice was strong and held conviction when he said, "My oath is also given, but how can you be sure this will be the end of it?"

"We will never be sure. We can only hope and pray, be more cautious about what we say, and have faith in those who are the keepers of this secret. This we can do," Vicente responded.

CHAPTER 27

The Final Chapter

A banquet was planned on the eve of the departure of General de Vallier. Although the Hacienda Escobedo was two days by coach from the Rancho Martinez and was a stop on the way back to Mexico City, Don Escobedo had sent word that he would be in attendance. He planned to accompany General de Vallier on the journey from Hacienda Martinez back to his home the next day.

"Come in," the door opened and Diego entered the General's room.

"I am sorry that you are leaving, sir," Diego said as the General dressed for the dinner being held in his honor.

"The trip across the Atlantic is hard and this is the best time to make it. I must return to attend to my station at the academy. I had hoped you might change your mind and become a student there."

"Sir, I am honored that you consider me worthy of acceptance, however I have spoken of this with my father and we feel it best for me to attend a University in the United States. We feel that the future of our nation is more closely aligned with the United States than it is with France. Please take no offence, sir."

"None is taken, young master Diego. I believe you are correct in your assessment. Enough said. How do I look?"

The General had on the dress uniform he had worn on the day of his arrival but had replaced the insignias of Colonel with those of a General.

"Magnificent. Only one thing is missing," Diego said as he stepped to the dresser, picked up the sword lying on it and presented it to the General, much like he had seen his mother do.

"Yes, thank you, sir," the General said, taking the sword and inserting it into the ring on his belt. "Now, I am ready to finish what I came here to do," he remarked, reaching into his large trunk.

"This is the last gift that needs to be given." He retrieved a parchment roll which was secured with three wax seals, one at each end and one in the center.

"Who is it for?" Diego asked.

"You must wait, so you can enjoy the presentation and be surprised with the others, young sir."

They left the General's quarters and went into the sala, where the guests were beginning to assemble.

General Escobedo arrived, leading an American and immediately sought out the company of the elder French statesman.

"General de Vallier, may I introduce to you, United States Ambassador to Mexico, Mr. Stanton. If you even notice me limping," Escobedo quipped to Stanton, "it's because De Vallier put a pistol ball into my leg during a little skirmish we had over near Pueblo a few years ago. They gave him one of these for doing it. Isn't that right?" Escobedo laughed as he tapped his white gloved finger against the gold and silver medals that adorned the Frenchman's tunic.

"How could I ever say it was not so, when you have such great pleasure from telling the story?" the distinguished gentleman chuckled fondly.

"If you will excuse me gentlemen," Escobedo stepped to where Vicente and Lupe were talking with other guests.

"I am very pleased to meet you, sir." The general shook the American's hand. "Diego, come here, young man. I would like you to meet this gentleman. Mr. Stanton, may I present Mr. Diego Martinez and inform you that he wishes to attend university in the United States, and may I suggest to you that he would make a fine cadet for your academy at West Point. It should be obvious to you that he would be a very valuable asset as your nation's ambitions unfold and take hold here in Mexico."

The American looked at the Frenchman with steely eyes, realizing the truth provided a defense against slander.

"If you would excuse me please," the General left Diego and the Ambassador to chat, making his way to Vicente.

"Would you call on me near the end of this evening? I have a few things that I would like to say."

"Of course. It will be a pleasure and honor." Vicente said.

When the moment arrived, Vicente stood and quieted the room.

"Our guest of honor wishes to have the floor. Sir," Vicente gestured toward the General.

De Valier rose and began, "I wish to thank our hosts for this fine party. The invitation called you to these festivities to honor me, but I must confess, I am not the one who should be honored among you. In fact, this evening I am merely a messenger," he said as he walked to the end of the table and stood next to Lupe.

"Guadalupe, this message is addressed to you. Would you please open it?" The General handed the parchment to Lupe. She slid her finger under the seals and opened the scroll.

"Merci, Madame," the General took the document from her, unrolled it, and began to read:

July 14, 1873 Versailles, France

Guadalupe Hidalgo Martinez, in recognition that your treatment of French troops as your prisoners of war exemplified the finest qualities of the human spirit, and in recognition of your courage under fire, exemplifying the finest qualities any country could ask of its soldier, I, Patrice de Mac-Mahon, President of the French Republic, bestow upon, Guadalupe Hidalgo Martinez, the French Legion of Honor Medal, the highest honor that I can bestow upon a soldier; furthermore, in recognition of all Mexican women who fought with vigor and courage, I order that your name appear on the Legion of Honor Tablet with the sub-inscription as follows,

"Guadalupe Hidalgo Martinez
La Soldada de Mexico"

ABOUT THE AUTHOR

Michael Black is a prolific writer and in addition to this book, is the author of *The Dream Merchant* and *Codey's Place.* His penchant for storytelling means that he is never finished writing about the volatility of the human condition.

When he's not traveling and writing, Michael can be found at his home in Clovis, California. You can see all his books and connect with him anytime at AuthorMichaelBlack.Yolasite.com.

MORE BY MICHAEL BLACK

The Dream Merchant

The enticement of easily obtained, richly vivid and infinitely diverse drea-ming on demand is something to die for—or kill for. On his journey to restore his sister's health, Jon Dean pursues a medical miracle—a DNA doorway. His path leads through adventures as unpredictable as recombining DNA. He must make a choice between wealth beyond imagination or the good of the whole.

Codey's Place

Love does not suffer from ignorance, injustice, or prejudice—but young lov-ers often do. Codey's Place chronicles the struggles of Christine, the white daug-hter of a plantation owner, and Codediah, the black son of the plantation manager. Born in segregated South Carolina, they must overcome societal traditions to fulfill their love. Can Codediah's uncompromising sense of his identity and understanding of his place in the world save their love from extinction?

9 781949 813111